"Erika Nichols-Frazer has written a dazzling collection of short stories that are sharp and cut deep. Her language is so lyrical and yet the stories of loss and love and delusion are heartbreaking in the best possible way. This is a writer who takes her time, who crafts every line even as she takes her reader into the depths, to the places where we all live."

—Mary Morris, author of *The Red House*

"In Erika Nichols-Frazer's beautifully crafted debut collection, *No One Will Ever Hear You*, we meet a host of characters who are struggling with ex-lovers, parents, current spouses, kids, coworkers, and their own bodies. Nichols-Frazer chooses an array of settings to tell her characters' stories, and those settings play a critically important role throughout. The unifying aspects of this impressive collection are her propulsive prose and pitch-perfect dialogue. A wonderful and memorable debut with relatable characters whose stories possess an enviable staying power."

—Keith Pilapil Lesmeister, author of *We Could've Been Happy Here*

"The characters at the center of these bracing stories tell their truths no matter how overwhelming the situations they face, and with a haunting beauty sometimes more suggestive of poetry than prose. Details tell all in these stories where spilt wine takes on layers of meaning, and you can smell and hear and see the worlds in which these people inhabit. Erika Nichol-Frazer has given us people to care deeply about, which is no small gift in our brutal world."

—Ken Harvey, author of *The Book of Casey Adair*

No One Will Ever Hear You

STORIES

ERIKA
NICHOLS-FRAZER

Rootstock Publishing
Montpelier, VT

Release Date: September 1, 2026

Paperback ISBN: 978-1-57869-230-9
Library of Congress Control Number: 2026940057

Published by Rootstock Publishing
an imprint of Ziggy Media, LLC
Montpelier, VT 05602
info@rootstockpublishing.com
www.rootstockpublishing.com

Cover Art: "Onward" original painting by Sally Stetson, acrylic on paper, 3' X 3' ©2016 SALLY STETSON.
Book formatting by Amit Dey (about.me/amitdey).

To Dylan, for always being here.
And to Arden, for making my life richer.

Contents

Ember

First, a whisper, chin stubble brushing cheek. You like how it feels to be wanted.

Quickly, the wildfires take the valley, swallowing it whole.

He didn't tell you at first, but you didn't ask. You didn't want to know that he was anything but yours.

A fire from the west meets a fire from the east—explodes. Up and down the coastline, everything burns.

He never says her name. She is only his wife. Nothing else. You don't know what you are.

It feels as though the drought has lasted your whole lifetime. You can barely remember days when you could run through the sprinkler, squealing, all afternoon until you were cooled off, no matter what day it was.

You meet during your lunch period. You park on an adjacent street, always in a different place. There is thrill in the precision of it.

The shape of a flame eating trees: The Eye of God.

The secret is hot in your belly.

You are evacuated from the only home you've ever lived in. You don't know if you'll see it again. Your mother gathers the good china and silver, which have been in the family for generations, as she likes to say, and fills a duffle bag with them. She pads it with wadded dinner napkins. She will keep her hands on the duffle bag at all times in the makeshift shelter in your high school gym.

Your mother told you recently, out of the blue, to guard your reputation, that it is the only real currency you have. You didn't know what to say to this.

You bring only the pearl necklace your grandmother gave you for your Sweet Sixteenth last year—the one she wore at her wedding—the baby blanket you were brought home in, now threadbare and faded from pink to a light gray, and your journal. You never used his name in it. Not once.

He won't leave his family for you. You know this.

He took his wife and daughter, who is only four years younger than you, to their house in the mountains. He hasn't texted to make sure you're alright. You decide that, even if he does, you won't respond.

Your mouth tastes like ash, your eyes teary from the sting of it.

You've never woken up with his face close to your face, his breath on your skin. These are the things you want but will not have.

The worst fire in over a century, the news says. The news is on everywhere. Homes like yours devastated, gone. Your neighbors,' where you went to Christmas and Fourth of July parties. Where living room couches and antique bedframes were, there is now nothing.

When he rolls away, he kisses your eyelids, his lips barely brushing them like the wings of a moth.

Can You Believe It?

"She seems to think she's one of the sow's own," the farmer tells me as he walks me out to the barn. My flats sink into the mud of the driveway and make a sucking sound with every step. Should've worn more farm-friendly shoes.

"Her mother was run over, so she's got nowhere else to feed." He adjusts his red Make America Great Again hat and opens the door for me. I imagine he'd be my dad's age, if my dad were still alive.

I follow him into the barn, down the aisle to the last stall, where a fat sow lounges, five piglets suckling at her side, and sure enough, a border collie pup. "Wouldn't you know it, just can't seem to convince her she ain't one of 'em," the farmer says. "We tried taking her away, feeding her the bottle, but she weren't having none of it."

I snap a few photos of the puppy amongst the piglets with the fancy camera one of the film guys showed me how to use. I'm terrified I'll break it. Chloe wouldn't ever let me touch her retro Nikon because, she said, I wasn't careful enough. I had a bad track record of dropping phones and spilling on laptops.

It's been a month since she left but she still hasn't picked up her framed photos, her desk, her records. The dress she always wore to weddings is still hanging in the closet. The second bedroom she used as an office/darkroom is still set up, as if she's coming back any day now, even though I know, this time, she's not.

Sometimes the "Can You Believe it?" segment I write at a satirical news show sends me out on location like this, if it's not too far from the city. Mostly, my work is done online, scanning small-town newspapers and social media. My search history would confound you.

The suckling pup upstate caught my boss Simone's attention. "It's the perfect photo op," she'd said. "A real, adorable, feel-good story! We need this." It had been a rough week, with another school shooting killing six children and a teacher, and a politician who was a proponent of gay conversion therapy discovered to have had a scandalous 'relationship' with an underage boy. A lot of ugliness. *I need it, too*, I thought.

"Are you fucking kidding me?" Chloe shouted, fuming. I'd left the door to the apartment unlocked, admittedly for the second time that month. "Do you know what could have happened, Meg? You do realize what neighborhood we're in, don't you? Remember Mrs. Alvarez down the hall? She got robbed last year! You don't need to give out a written invitation!"

"I'm sorry," I said, though my heart wasn't in it. She always found something to criticize these days and I was sick of apologizing for leaving the last swig of milk in the fridge or my hair clogging the shower drain. She was quick to anger, and I didn't like the person I'd become around her, this compliant, apologetic woman always admitting defeat.

I slept on the couch with our dog that night and googled more news.

A pagan sect in Spain claimed to have cured cancer by praying and conducting rituals to expel the sickness from the body.

"I could feel the cancer leaving me, like this presence, this weight, lifting off of me," one of the cured said in the article I found on a Pagan website. The leader, or "healer," as her followers called her, was part-shaman, part-priest, no doctor. And yet, doctors in a nearby clinic confirmed the woman's inexplicably sudden remission after they'd given her three months to live. The followers, of course, took this as proof and worshipped with devotion. I wish I could believe in something like that.

A man in Massachusetts found his wedding ring around a carrot he plucked from the soil. He'd lost it ten years ago, apparently in the garden. He and his wife of thirty-seven years were ecstatic. I have a soft spot for the feel-good ones, though Simone prefers the salacious stuff, crimes and affairs and corruption. But the fluffy stories get more tweets, so she gives in. Surfing pigs, triplets reunited after thirty years, that sort of thing.

I know Chloe's been stressed at her job at a medical supply company, passed over for another promotion. It's sexism, she says, the way they treat her, *and* homophobia. I've heard the rant on repeat, picking up speed and tenacity as she drinks. Still, she doesn't need to take her frustration out on me.

Simone took the staff out for drinks one night at a trendy hipster bar in the village. Chloe hardly spoke the whole night, nursed her drinks sullenly, so unlike her usual, animated self.

It was past midnight and we were waiting for the F-train, Chloe swaying a little in that way that's a telltale sign she's had a few too many.

"OK, I know you're pissed at me for some reason," I said. "You might as well get it out."

"Are you fucking her?" she asked, looking past me.

"Who?"

"Who do you think? Simone!"

"You think I'm fucking my boss? That's bullshit."

"You barely even looked at me all night!"

"That's not fair, I was just being polite—"

"I may as well not even have been there."

"Well, stay home next time, then!"

She was silent for a while and wouldn't look me in the eye.

"I'm going to catch an Uber. I'll see you at home," she said, and turned from the platform toward the exit. I didn't go after her. I realized I didn't want to. When I got home, she'd packed a bag. She didn't tell me where she was going.

A man in Indianapolis was arrested for public drunkenness after trying to use a mailbox as an ATM. Simone found this one hilarious, delivered some well-received jokes about it. "Another drunk dude can't find the slot," I'd written.

Simone insisted something was wrong—she said I looked pale as a porcelain doll and "bedraggled"—until I relented and told her about Chloe leaving. She was sympathetic, though I could tell she was getting off on it. She likes to be important, always the center of attention. She sees herself as infinitely wise. It's her gift, she says. She calls it that on the show, "her gift," knowing. An empath, she likes to say. She'd been through a public break-up a few months earlier, with a soap opera actor, which was splashed all over the tabloids. I will admit, though she can be a hard-ass, she was pretty supportive about the Chloe thing and even brought me a coffee and a Morning Glory muffin the day after I told her. I didn't have the heart to tell her I can't eat gluten.

Back in college, I thought I would be like Simone, a stand-up comedian and host of one of the most popular satirical news shows on prime time. When we were first going out, Chloe encouraged me to do a few open mic nights, but I was passable at best. Standing on stage made me nervous, though Chloe's presence and support almost made me believe in myself. After a few lukewarm performances, it was clear my stand-up career was going nowhere and, when she saw the ad in the paper, Chloe told me I just *had* to apply for the staff writer position. It's where I belong, anyway, behind the scenes. You don't see many fat women on prime time.

"You're just big-boned," my mother insisted when I was in eighth grade and came home crying after Marissa Stevens called me a whale in gym class. "And you have such a pretty face." I did slim down as I grew up, but I still shop at Lane Bryant.

Though Chloe was fit, a runner, she never made me feel unattractive, never used my body against me. She was the first person who made me feel wanted. Peter, my ex-fiancé, gifted me a Weight Watchers membership once we got engaged, said didn't I want to fit into my wedding dress? But Chloe regularly called me beautiful, sexy. She made me feel seen.

We met at the marathon when she was running and I was volunteering. A friend whose wife was competing had dragged me along. She'd pointed out that I needed to get more involved in things, engage, give back. I had nothing to say to this, so I got up at 5:00 a.m. on an eighteen-degree Sunday in November to check in runners and hand out water. I was staffing the refreshments tent as runners finished. Chloe made pretty good time and, even while wrapped in a blanket and red-faced, managed to brag while flirting with me. Here was this stunning woman whose sharp features, even sweaty, were striking, her long blonde hair in a tight ponytail. She was confident, strong, everything I didn't feel like. We went to the farmers' market in Union Square and the Strand the next weekend. We started spending every spare moment together and I moved into her apartment on the Lower East Side just a few months later.

Other than when she occasionally traveled to conferences for work, I hadn't slept without her in three years. I always slept with my back to her, her right arm draped over my hip, possessing me. There was a sturdiness to her, a trustworthiness. She took care of me, even if she did try to make decisions for me. That was its own kind of love.

Who gets to keep Mork, our German Shepherd? We adopted him last year, convinced we had a long relationship ahead of us, imagining years of walks and dog parks and throwing sticks. He's become attached to me, the one who usually gets home at a reasonable hour and feeds him. I guess since Chloe moved out, I get the apartment. I'll have to get a roommate; I can't afford it by myself. I don't want to live with some rando. Who keeps the car? She does, I'm sure, since she drives to work in midtown while I take the F-train to work. Anyway, she took it with her. I didn't let myself look out of the window, at her, with armfuls of her shit; didn't watch her go.

A woman drove her Rav-4 into Lake Michigan because her GPS told her to turn right. Simone loved that one. It felt good to make someone happy. I realized Chloe hadn't made me happy in a long time.

The final straw came one night when I'd had to work late; another show had done the story I'd put together about a woman who ran for thirty days straight, from one side of the country to another. Simone found that boring, and came into the writing room in a fury shortly before I was planning on leaving to meet Chloe for dinner at a Georgian restaurant whose owner we'd befriended. Chloe's good at making the kind of friends you say hi to but not the kind whom you text. She's good at being friendly, but not at being vulnerable. The truth is, she doesn't really have friends of her own. So, when Simone stormed in and demanded that I come up with a new story for the night's show, *stat*, I texted Chloe that I couldn't make dinner. No response.

When I got home, she was sitting at the kitchen table, nursing a whiskey, which, judging by the way she was slumped in her chair, wasn't her first. She was clearly pissed and I didn't want to engage and get in another argument. I was rooting through the fridge for leftovers when she finally spoke.

"I know you've been hooking up with her," she said, ice-cold. "Don't lie to me."

"I'm not doing this," I said, a take-out container of veggie fried rice in one hand, a block of cheddar cheese in the other. "If you don't trust me, how is this supposed to work?"

"I guess it doesn't work anymore," she said. She paused before saying, "I saw the text."

"What text?"

"The one she sent you in the middle of the night."

"I can't believe you looked at my phone."

"And I can't believe you're fucking cheating on me!"

"Nothing happened. We haven't done anything."

"It doesn't matter. You obviously want her more than you want me."

"That's ridiculous. I—"

"I don't want to hear it. I'm getting a hotel room. I'm done."

I had never been in a relationship with a woman before Chloe. Peter and I got engaged shortly out of college, though that engagement only lasted a few months before I realized I wasn't in love with him, no matter how much I wanted to be. After that, I didn't really date anyone for a few years.

The first time I hooked up was at a friend's bachelorette party with a woman in the bar bathroom. She propped me up on the sink, getting my skirt wet from the dripping faucet, and went down on me. I'd never done anything like that before, in a public place, and certainly wouldn't have sober. There were a few other friends-of-friends in my early twenties, but it never went beyond hooking up a handful of times before it fizzled out, or, usually, I stopped returning their calls or texts. I was afraid of losing myself in another relationship. And then I met Chloe. She liked to sing karaoke (she had "I Will Survive" down) and volunteered mentoring LGBTQ+ youth. She wasn't like the self-deprecating, struggling actors and comedians and writers I hung out with. She was driven, organized, determined. I wanted to be as strong as she was.

Chloe hadn't spoken to her parents since high school. They apparently didn't handle her coming out well. "It's the Bible belt," she shrugged when we first talked about it over coffee, but I could tell she didn't dismiss it as easily as she pretended to.

It wasn't until we were living together and I jumped in the shower with her one morning that I saw the horizontal scars on her wrists. I ran my fingers over them. She pulled away but I told her it didn't matter, that I loved her, that she was worthy of love. It had been years since she'd done it, she said, but she needed a release after her parents kicked her out of the house, needed some control, and seeing how much she could handle hurt eased the pain of loneliness.

"Have you ever tried to get back in touch with your parents?" I asked over breakfast one time.

She fiddled with the spoon in her latte. "My dad said he was ashamed of me, that he had no daughter. I don't think they want to hear from me."

My mother practically adopted Chloe once she met her. She knit her a scarf every Christmas and texted her regularly. She did her best to be the parent Chloe was missing, and I loved my mom for that. Chloe knew my mom had a weird thing for elephants and often gave her things with elephants on them: mugs and cards and t-shirts, which were scattered throughout her house. I didn't want to think about how my mom would take it when I told her Chloe had left.

The farmer invites me in for a cup of coffee and a slice of apple pie his wife made. "Best apple pie in the state," he brags. "Our own apples, o' course."

I have nothing in common with these people. A child of the suburbs, now a liberal city-dweller, and an older couple who live in an 1800s farmhouse adorned with American flags. We talk about our dogs and how bad the traffic is in the city.

"Wouldn't want my kids to live in the big city," the farmer says with a mouth full of pie, wiping apple from his whiskered chin. "Bad influence, you ask me."

"It's alright," I say, taking delicate bites of the flaky crust, savoring each bite. I can't remember the last time I had homemade pie.

"All those drug addicts and loose women," he shakes his head, "Criminals, gays; it's not safe for a nice young girl like you."

I nearly choked on my pie. What was I supposed to say to that? I'm one of those "gays" you're so afraid of?

"Sam, you always find the worst in everything," the farmer's wife, a petite woman with long hair in braids piled atop her head, softly scolds, pouring more coffee into his mug without asking. She changes the subject and asks me if I'm married. I hesitate, consider lying, then say I just went through a break-up.

"You'll find the right man," the woman assures me.

"I'm not looking for a man," I say, trying to hold back the fury in my voice.

I can't see myself with a man ever again, though, of course, at this point it's hard to picture myself with anyone but Chloe. I'm not even sure if it's her I want back, or the life we built together, a life that made sense. I knew who I'd have dinner with every night (takeout, more often than not), who I would tell about my day, Simone's latest antics, something strange I'd come across in my research. She reminded me to pay bills and clean the lint out of the dryer and a thousand other things that might otherwise slip my mind. She kept me grounded, tethered, and now I feel as if I'm floating away.

I don't want to be a person who defines themselves by their relationships, who changes for the person they're with. I want to be stronger than that, want to take control for once.

"One thing I love about the city is there aren't as many homophobes as in a small town like this," I said, taking another mouthful of pie. They're both silent, unblinking.

Eventually, the farmer kisses his wife on the cheek as he gets up to muck stalls and shakes my hand. "Good, strong handshake," he says, and I can't help but feel flattered, as if this man were someone I want to impress. He seems like what I'd imagine a father to be, strong, dependable, I think maybe a bit strict. There is a gruffness to this guy, a sharpness in his tone, but affection, too. There are framed pictures of grown kids with grandkids all over the fading papered walls, children's brightly colored drawings on the fridge.

I had to borrow Simone's Mercedes for the trip upstate, since Chloe still has our car and I couldn't ask her to borrow it. She hasn't reached out since she left and I don't want to be the first. I'm not great with a stick shift (despite my mom having insisted on teaching me), so the car rumbles and jolts every time I have to switch gears as dirt roads turn to school zones, and I stall out on a hill and am grateful there are no cars behind me. Every song that my phone shuffles through reminds me of Chloe.

I don't like to be alone. And now, about to turn thirty, I don't know myself on my own, don't know how to move forward.

I read somewhere that it's common for women who go through a break-up to change their appearance, their clothes, most often their hair. While I don't want to be a stereotype, this seems like a pretty good idea, so I go to a salon I've never been to and ask them to dye my hair pink. It's bolder than my usual look, my brown hair in a pixie cut and dark, baggy clothes. I want to be someone Chloe wouldn't recognize.

She wasn't all ultimatums and drunken jealousy. She was fresh flowers and my favorite pizza every Friday, arm around my shoulders, holding me close as we watched the movie that she always let me pick, running her fingers through my hair, scrambled eggs on Sunday mornings. She was warmth and protection and someone who cared what I did. Now the only one who cares if I come home is Mork, and only because he wants his dinner.

A man in India claims he can live on air alone. He calls himself a "breatharian." He gets very little physical exercise but breathes mindfully all day long. He hasn't eaten or drunk anything in forty-four days. Doctors declare this medically impossible. Already, he's amassed thousands of followers. They assume he must be holy, to survive like that. I can understand the want to believe. I want not to need, not to hunger. I want to learn to just *be*, on my own terms. I want a purpose, a meaning, someone who cares if I'm alive. To breathe. To be remembered.

Anything Good

My mother doesn't usually just drop by like this. She lives across town, but we only see each other for the occasional dinner and it's been a while. I'm not sure what she's doing here.

I pick up mouse turds from the kitchen counter with a paper towel and toss them in the trash before she notices. I'll set a trap once she leaves. Jake usually deals with that kind of thing. I can't stomach the limp bodies halved by the bloody metal. The best you can hope for is a clean kill.

"Someone stole Ruthie's hosta," Mom says from the living room. I know she's inspecting the photographs on the bookshelf, examining the curated version of our lives. Most of the photos are of Aubrey alone; Aubrey as a baby on her belly, Aubrey as a toddler with her favorite stuffed dragon, a collection of school photos of her, gap-toothed and smiling. The most recent photo is of her and Jake at the lake last summer, her on his shoulders in the water, before they fell. At ten, she's getting too big for that kind of thing now. The only photo of Jake and me is from our wedding, dancing to "Endless Love."

"What?" I call back.

"That plant thief who's been digging up people's gardens all over town. This is the third time this month."

I take two mugs of coffee in one hand, by the handles—one black and one bone-white, the way she likes it—and a plate of two-day-old zucchini bread in the other.

"It's nice out; let's sit on the porch," I say.

I don't need her commentary on the unfolded laundry on the couch. I'd planned to do it this morning, but Aubrey wouldn't do a thing I asked her to do, so we were late to Girl Scout camp. A few drips of coffee slosh onto the porch as I set the mugs down on the wicker table.

"You spilled a little, sweetie." She points, lowering her long, lean body onto the wicker couch. I wipe the coffee away with my bare foot.

"I hope you clean the rest of the house better than that." She takes a sip and smacks her lips. She just can't resist the opportunity. This is why I put off her attempts to get together.

"Move over." I sit down next to her. "What was that about being hostile?"

"Hmmm?"

"I don't know, couldn't hear you. You said something about hostile."

"Oh, no. *Hosta.* You know, the plant with the big leaves. The one in my shade garden? You remember my friend Ruthie?"

"Yeah, the one who kept flirting with Jake's college friends at our wedding."

"She called this morning. She gets up at dawn to walk her dog, this yappy little thing she takes everywhere. When they walked out this morning, there was a big gaping hole in her garden. One of her hostas was missing! Stolen! They left the other two."

Through a mouth full of stale zucchini breadcrumbs I ask, "Are you sure it's not some kind of animal? A raccoon, maybe?"

She scoffs and reaches for a slice of bread. A diamond tennis bracelet rattles around her bony wrist. The jewelry she's wearing right now is worth more than I make in a year, I'm sure.

"It was too neat to be an animal, a perfectly round hole. She said you could tell it had been dug up with tools—lifted right out, roots and all." She frowns a little as she chews.

I have to crane my head to see the clock in the living room behind her. A little less than an hour before I have to pick up Aubrey. When I dropped her off this morning, she told me I'd better not be late to pick her up again and reminded me "Dad's always on time." Sometimes she's more like Jake than I can stand. She thinks he's coming back any day now. He told her he was going on a trip for work and wouldn't be long. He told me he needed some space, ten days ago. He's called to talk to her every day, but we haven't spoken more than a few words. He's been leaving for a long time. So long, most of him was already gone.

"Besides," my mother says, a smear of chocolate chip on her bright-red lip, "an animal would've left tracks. Dragged the thing. It wouldn't have just lifted it up and disappeared."

I grab Jake's binoculars from the windowsill behind her head. He likes to sit out here and watch birds. There are three bird books on the side table, but he doesn't need them. He knows the name of every bird in North America. Aubrey has memorized his books and shouts out names constantly in the car. *Sparrow! Chickadee! Crow!*

"What are you looking at?" Mom asks.

"Remember that time the bear took our compost?"

"That's what happens when you leave rotting food out."

"We didn't *leave it out.* That's what compost is—decomposing food scraps. It was in a bin."

"Basically gift-wrapped for him."

"Well, that thing's heavy. I can't even spin it on my own. And he—she, I don't know—just picked it up like it was a toy and walked right off with it."

"A bear didn't take Ruthie's hosta. Or a raccoon or any other animal, for that matter. I bet it was a drug addict."

I choke on my coffee and dribble some onto my t-shirt. "Why would you say that?"

"Who else would steal someone's plants? Drug addicts steal anything."

"I don't think someone on drugs would go through all the trouble of digging up a stranger's plants in the middle of the night. What would they do with it, anyway?"

"You never know. They do all kinds of crazy things."

My mother puts her half-eaten bread back on the plate.

"So how's my Aubrey doing? Is she loving camp?"

"She's fine. She likes seeing her friends, but I'm not sure she's as into the Girl Scout thing anymore."

"Well, she has just about every badge she could get by now, right?"

"Something like that."

I look through the binoculars but see only sky.

"Are you coming over for Easter dinner?" my mother asks.

"Since when do we celebrate Easter?"

"You don't have to be religious to celebrate Easter. I used to make a lamb roast every year. And we went to that egg hunt at the church when you were a kid."

"I don't remember that."

"We did lots of stuff like that when you were little. You never remember anything good."

I remember lots of good things, I want to say. I remember when Aubrey was tiny, so fragile, how she loved to curl into the curve of my body, how she needed me. I remember when Jake couldn't keep his hands off me, making love on this porch in the middle of the day.

"So, are you coming?"

The last thing I want right now is to endure a formal dinner at my mother's house.

"I guess Aubrey and I can. Jake has to travel for work." It's true often enough that the excuse seems plausible. I know I won't be able to handle her feedback on my marriage. Until I know for sure, she and Aubrey can both go on thinking he's on another work trip.

She takes a long sip of coffee. "I don't know how long it's been since I've seen him. Months. You only live twenty minutes away."

I turn away from her. "He works a lot."

"Well, he can still make time for family. Are you sure everything's all right?"

I picked up his disposable razor in the medicine cabinet the other day, looking for mine, and had to lock myself in the bathroom for half an hour so I could cry without Aubrey seeing me.

"Fine, Mom."

"How's Aubrey handling things?"

"She's fine. We're both fine. There's nothing to handle."

"I could watch her next weekend, if you want. So you and Jake can have some alone time."

"He'll still be away. But thanks." I hope she doesn't hear the quiver in my voice.

A small black dot hovers above the trees behind our house. A hawk, I think. Through the binoculars I scan the overcast sky for it. My mother huffs but doesn't say anything. Definitely a hawk, circling in slow, patient loops, hunting the forest. Are our chickens secure in their coop? Jake has chastised me a million times for forgetting to lock them in, but yes, Aubrey noticed one on top of our fence when we were about to leave this morning, and she put her back and locked them all up.

"You know you can talk to me." We don't look at each other. "I left your father once." She takes my silence as an invitation to continue. "Years ago. You were too little to remember."

"I was little? You mean you left me, too?"

"Only for a few days. I came back. That's my point."

The hawk circles above us. It waits. I would give it the mice, if I could. I would offer a sparrow, a chickadee, a crow. I would carve a perfect hole and lift my heart out, roots and all.

Table For One

The place looked nothing like it did the last time Frank was here. The lights were dimmer and the dining car had been carpeted, no more squeaky linoleum floors. It had looked pretty much the same on the outside, metal boxcar, a bit worse for the wear. The sign no longer said "Diner" in blinking neon lights but was an understated painted deal that said "Trattoria," which Frank wasn't sure how to pronounce.

The old booths had been replaced with round tables with white linens. The walls were covered with black-and-white photographs of Worcester in the early 1900s, around the time Frank's grandparents emigrated. The photos showed carriages on dirt roads when downtown was just a few two-story buildings, long before the restaurant was surrounded by office buildings and a condo complex.

He had an inkling to turn right back out the door and make sure he'd gone into the right place. The diner was no longer itself. He was pretty sure it couldn't be called a diner anymore. Diners have fried food and greasy eggs and at least two kinds of pie. Diners don't have white tablecloths or vases of white roses. It wouldn't have been unlike him to go to the wrong place. He was getting more forgetful these days, turning the house upside down looking for the glasses on his head, misplacing his keys three or four times whenever he got ready to go out. His body and mind seemed to have deteriorated rapidly in the past six months. Everything took more effort than it once had.

Decades of building houses had worn down his joints and torn his muscles. He had gotten too old to swing a hammer all day, his back tired and stiff, the years of hard labor unforgiving. He'd still managed to pick up a few odd maintenance jobs but had given them up when Lynn got sick. Now, his body sagged with grief, back hunched and knees shaking with the weight he bore on his own.

Frank could still smell the grease from the fry-o-lator and hear Roy Orbison on the jukebox. He wouldn't have been surprised to see a young Lynn bump the kitchen door open with her hip, hands filled with trays of fries and frappes, winking when she spotted him and bringing him a hot cup of coffee and a slice of cherry pie without having to be asked. But of course, there was no pie and no Lynn. This wasn't that kind of place anymore. And he was no longer a twenty-something bachelor who came in for pie and drank six cups of coffee every day at the New Englander so he could talk to the cute waitress. He wasn't sure what would have been worse: the restaurant bearing no resemblance to the diner where he first saw her, or the place looking the same without her.

"Are you on your own tonight, sir?" the hostess asked. He nodded and was led to a table, where she removed the other napkin, water glass, and silverware.

Today would have been their fiftieth anniversary. Technically, he supposed, it was still their anniversary, even though she wasn't here to celebrate it with him. It was still their day. They had celebrated most of their anniversaries at home with steak and chocolate cake—the only times she made the kind not from a box—but he'd only learned to make himself a few basic things since she'd died and none of them was steak or not-from-a-box chocolate cake. Mostly these days, his diet was a reliable mix of frozen Hungry Man meals, boxed macaroni and cheese, and hot dogs he cooked in a pan with a fork. Lynn probably wouldn't have won any awards for her cooking—her food never looked like it did on the cooking shows she watched—but he liked it just fine. What he wouldn't give for her lasagna, or roast, or just about anything, really, a hot meal freshly cooked with her hands. She hadn't had much energy for cooking in the last few months, and they ate a lot of canned soups and things like mashed potato flakes and frozen vegetables. She didn't care much for hot dogs, even when they went to Fenway. Frank and Tim always had to get two Fenway Franks each or the Sox would lose, guaranteed.

The walk four blocks through downtown Worcester had made him thirsty and he downed most of his ice-cold water in one loud slurp. Diners glanced, but he stared only at the empty chair across from him. He saw Lynn there, in the blue dress she wore whenever they went somewhere fancy, which wasn't often. Dining out had been a special-occasion-only event for Frank and Lynn. When they did, it wasn't at fancy restaurants like this. They couldn't afford that kind of luxury. Frank certainly can't afford it now, but that wasn't going to stop him from celebrating the way Lynn would have wanted. They'd never had much extra money lying around and, on the rare occasion when they ate out, his constant complaining about prices and portion sizes and having to tip would make the whole experience no more pleasant than cooking and doing the dishes at home.

The image he saw in front of him was not of the wilted Lynn who lay in a hospital bed, but Lynn before the cancer took her full, flushed cheeks and silver curls. He imagined her tucking a loose strand of hair behind her ear, fiddling with the necklace she wore every day, the one he'd gotten her for a birthday or anniversary years ago—she was always fiddling, doing something with her hands.

Lynn was never a big baseball fan, not nearly as faithful as Frank and Tim, but she was at every game Tim ever played in, and she always came along to cheer for the Sox, even if she did complain about the traffic and drunks jostling her or yelling right in her ears. Every time she whined, Frank would tell her she could stay home if she preferred, but she immediately repented. He understood. Looking back, a lot of his best memories of Tim were at ball games.

Even the time when Tim was nine and he caught a foul ball—never failed to bring his mitt, just in case, although that was the only time he actually got to use it—but he caught it too close to his face and the speed and force of the thing knocked it right into Tim's mouth, hard. Two of his bottom teeth were broken and blood was everywhere, dribbled down his chin, neck, and onto the collar of his Little League t-shirt. Tim didn't want to leave the game to go to the hospital. *But, Dad, we're tied at the bottom of the eighth!* he'd said, a mouthful of Red Sox logo napkins wrapped around ice from Lynn's soda. *At least it was only baby teeth*, she said more than once, as if that made it easier to leave with the bases loaded.

Forks and knives screeched across porcelain plates. Glasses clinked against each other and settled hard onto tablecloths. Frank had nothing he could do with his hands. His water was already gone.

Then there was a young man at his side, so tall that Frank had to crane his neck to look up at him, which strained his muscles. This lanky kid was Tim, bent over towards him with his hands folded behind his back. Tim as he would have looked at age nineteen or twenty, brown hair shaggy and unkempt, longer than Tim ever wore it. The eyes, though, were strikingly similar, the kind of green that reminded Frank of the kaleidoscope in his grandfather's study, which he would squint into and turn slowly as a child, shattering stained-glass masterpieces and forming new ones, over and over. Even now, he could remember clearly seeing those gray-blue glassy eyes of his newborn son and how they made him think of that leather-wrapped kaleidoscope, shards of blue slowly turning to green.

Not-Tim introduced himself as Riley, his server. He listed off specials too quickly, mostly words Frank didn't recognize, words that sounded Italian, foods he was pretty sure he'd never eaten. The server set a menu in front of Frank and pointed to the wine list open in the center of the table. Another boy, this one in a plain black shirt, refilled Frank's water glass. Riley said something Frank didn't catch and walked away. Frank was sorry to see him go. He wanted to ask him to sit down with him, tell him about what it was like to be whatever-age-he-was. Did he go to college? He looked college aged. Maybe he went somewhere nearby, to Clark or Poly Tech, maybe Holy Cross.

The glass sweated onto the tablecloth. A puddle spread from the base like an ink blot. Frank reached for the leather-bound wine list, which was two inches thick. He flipped through heavy paper made to look old and faded. Long foreign words scrawled in cursive with exotic places listed next to them. He couldn't remember the kind of wine she liked. *Syrah? Or was it Merlot?* Whatever it was, she kept big bottles of it behind the towels in the linen closet, and he pretended not to know about them. He asked for a bottle of red.

Frank picked up the menu, two pages of foods that he mostly didn't recognize, many of them not even in English. There were no prices listed next to anything. It seemed like a pretty big oversight to have left the prices off. He wondered if he should ask for another menu. He looked around at the other diners, seemingly unconcerned and enjoying their meals. Were these the kind of people who didn't care what things cost, didn't even ask? Maybe they had no idea what the price of a meal should be; maybe they just signed on the dotted line and didn't even look at the numbers on the bill. Frank knew his numbers.

He knew he had ninety-seven dollars left in his bank account, which he also knew was not enough. He knew his mortgage was due next week. He knew he hadn't worked in over a year and had few to no prospects for changing that. Zero: the number of living family members to whom he could reach out. Neither he nor Lynn had spoken to her sister in years, save for the Christmas card she still sent every year of her perfectly photogenic family, kids still alive and growing, grandkids whose names Frank could never remember.

Since a Marine had stood in uniform on their front stoop and rang the doorbell to destroy their lives, Frank and Lynn had drifted through the next two decades like two planets in different orbits, moving apart so slowly it was barely noticeable. The air between them settled into a stubborn kind of silence. Neither of them was the same without Tim. It was as though they shrank with the loss, became something less than their whole selves. Still, they went on walks together almost every day, at first just to get her to go outside, but they never stopped. They rarely touched but walked beside each other comfortably.

Tim had been scouted by several schools his senior year, and Frank had hoped he'd play right here in Worcester. Wherever he chose, Frank and Lynn were both determined to see every baseball game, even if he sat on the bench the whole game. Dinnertimes during Tim's senior year were mostly spent talking about where Tim would go, that is, where he would play, which teams were worthy of his curve ball. Tim was good but he wasn't MLB good, or farm team good—at least not yet—so he and Frank spent a lot of evenings getting in extra pitching practice in the backyard.

Frank wasn't sure exactly what changed his son's mind. He'd loved baseball his whole life, was a reasonably decent student, if a little lazy when it came to studying, but certainly could have gotten a college degree, unlike both of his parents. The first rejection letter hit him hard, and by the third, he stopped mentioning them to his parents. He stopped talking about college, when and where he'd play.

One night at dinner, he announced he was enlisting. A different type of recruiter than the ones at his baseball games had visited his high school and convinced their son that it was his duty to defend his country, that's what Tim told them. He had a duty. Frank had fought in a war, too; he knew about duty. He had fought so his son could have something better. He hadn't enlisted; those were the days of the draft. Had he had the money or the grades to even think about college, he would have gone, anywhere instead of Viet Nam. But he didn't tell Tim this. He didn't say anything. Lynn begged him not to go and it didn't make a bit of difference. Their son died in a war that most Americans didn't even remember.

The server had returned with a wine bottle and struggled with the corkscrew, digging into it at an awkward angle, bits of cork crumbling to the ground. The cork released with a loud *pop* and a splash of red wine onto Frank's chest.

"Oh my God, I'm so sorry," the kid sputtered. He set the open bottle and corkscrew on the table and used the white handkerchief folded over his arm to dab Frank's chest.

"No, no," Frank flailed his arms to ward off the kid, who kept trying to blot away the stain, spreading purple blooms over Frank's white shirt. He tried to lean away from the boy and his chair tipped back. He caught himself before he fell, but pulled the tablecloth towards him, sending his silverware and empty water glass onto the floor. Heads all over the room turned towards the commotion.

The server, Riley, looked at Frank, eyes questioning. Before he could answer, Frank started to laugh. Uncontrollable, snorting laughs.

A short man in a suit came over, introduced himself as the manager, and offered the bottle of wine on the house, which only set Frank off again.

Nearby diners turned back to their meals. The server stood next to Frank, waiting for him to do something. Frank's laughter subsided and he wiped away the tears forming in his eyes with his napkin, then tossed it, crumpled, onto the table.

"Really, Tim, don't worry about it." The boy's eyebrow raised in question. "Riley, sorry, I meant Riley. Forget the shirt."

"I just hope it's not ruined."

"Wouldn't matter if it was. I've had this shirt for fifty years and I don't plan on wearing it again."

As the boy in the black t-shirt laid down a new tablecloth and reset the table, Riley picked up the bottle of wine and resumed the ceremony. The cloth he was supposed to hold the bottle with was still in his hand, splattered with wine. He stuffed it in his pocket and poured the bottle into Frank's glass, a little shaky. Frank gestured to him in a silent "cheers," and took a big swig. He smacked his lips a few times, sipped again, and set the glass down. No sniffing and swirling. No comments about the notes or undertones. Riley asked how it tasted.

"Just fine. I'm not really much of a wine drinker," Frank admitted, "In case you hadn't guessed. It was more of my wife's drink. But I figured you probably don't serve Narragansett."

Riley smiled, his body relaxing a little. "You're right, there. So, you ready to order?"

"I almost forgot about it for a minute there."

"So, what'll you have?"

"Oysters…and the veal *ca-cacki-*"

"*Cacciatore*," Riley mercifully finished for him, with a smile turning up his lips.

Frank nodded and put the menu down on the table. Riley leaned over to pick it up and went to place the order. Frank inspected the stain on his shirt. It looked like a bloated heart. It was his only good button-up and he'd worn it to both his son's and wife's funerals. It was more off-white than white these days. Even in it, he looked underdressed for the restaurant; all the other men wore sports jackets and ties.

Lynn would have insisted they go home immediately so she could douse the shirt in club soda before the stain set, even if she knew he would never wear it again. She would not have been able to let it go and enjoy a meal in a fine restaurant the rest of the evening with Frank looking like a mess. He, however, had little interest in his appearance.

The oysters arrived with a quick "Enjoy," and his server rushed to another table, looking a bit flustered. Frank hadn't noticed the tables filling in around him. Suddenly the place was full.

He picked up an oyster shell between his thumb and pointer finger, dripping a little of the juice onto his lap, and sucked the thing down. He coughed, surprised by the slimy way it slid down his throat. He'd never cared much for oysters, but they were Lynn's favorite. After half a century, he felt he owed her a good meal.

He watched the other diners as he chewed. A young woman rubbed her foot up her date's leg while twirling her pasta. A boy squirmed in his seat, flicking red sauce all over the tablecloth, his parents ignoring him as they sipped their wine. A father sliced his small daughter's chicken, holding the fork out for her to wrap her lips around a piece that looked too big for her. Two serious men in starched suits chewed their meat, not talking or making eye contact. Frank turned back to the empty chair across from him.

He could see her smile, the way she rolled her eyes and pretended to be exasperated by him. Though Tim's death had left a distance between them, he still knew her, knew the way she hummed Beatles songs when she thought no one was listening, the way she rubbed his shoulders when she wanted sex. He knew her better than anybody and now she was gone.

The veal was good, tender, soft as butter in his mouth. Lynn probably would've protested about the poor baby cows. She had a soft spot for animals. Tim's allergies had kept them from having a dog when he was young, and there didn't seem much point to it after he was gone. But Lynn would've adopted every stray she could if she'd had her say.

His server returned, red-faced and slightly out of breath, and asked if he wanted dessert, coffee, an after-dinner drink. Normally, Frank would decline, but he wasn't eager to end his meal. He ordered a Grand Marnier, an espresso (not entirely certain of what it was), and tiramisu. It was the cake Lynn chose for their wedding. Her parents hadn't had much money, either, but they paid for the wedding, a small, simple affair, and the cake was one thing Lynn refused to skimp on. He never told her he thought tiramisu tasted like a dish sponge soaked in coffee. He had still eaten a bite of it from her hands.

Frank lifted his wineglass and toasted the empty chair. "Happy anniversary, Lynnie," he whispered. He took a bite of the cake. A little bitter for his taste.

Riley asked if he wanted anything else, and when Frank couldn't think of anything more he might possibly want, Riley placed the black leather folder with the bill inside. Frank swallowed hard before he looked. He knew what he was risking coming here. He knew this was his final act, the last of his money, that no more would be coming in. Frank had never been the kind of person to rely on others and had little patience for them. Up until very recently, Frank had criticized people who lived outside their means, who dug their own financial graves. And yet here he sat, licking whipped cream from tiramisu from a silver fork, a bill he was afraid to look at sitting in front of him.

Sipping the last of his Grand Marnier, Frank let the liquor warm his mouth. The tiny espresso cup was empty; he had downed the strong coffee in a few quick gulps, with two spoonsful of sugar. He'd left the cake mostly untouched.

When he finally got up the nerve to look at the bill, it felt like his heart stopped. $127, even without the wine. Too much. He had been prepared for this anniversary meal without Lynn—the only gift he could think of to give her now—to end his savings. There were no pensions or retirement plans, his social security check sunk into the mortgage and bills, no 401Ks or IRAs, no investments or assets to speak of. The insurance hadn't covered all of Lynn's treatments; his meager savings were gone. The house would be taken, he knew. He had figured his last ninety-seven dollars wasn't nearly enough to save his house from being foreclosed upon or to change his circumstances. But he hadn't expected that it wasn't even enough to enjoy a good anniversary meal. Not even close.

He suddenly felt was if everyone in the restaurant was staring at him, which, of course they weren't, because an old man by himself was sort of sad, but not particularly remarkable. That, he thought, was likely to change quickly. What happened to old men who couldn't pay their tabs? Would the police get involved? What could they do, slap a fine on him that he couldn't pay, either? Would he be banned from the restaurant? Arrested? Lynn would be so embarrassed. He tried not to see her sitting there with him anymore, shaking her head, disapproval in her eyes. He wanted to apologize—to her, to the restaurant, to Riley, to Tim, to everyone. He couldn't find the words.

Then a terrible thought occurred to him. Would Riley be punished for his inability to pay? Would the bill come out of his paycheck? He looked so much like Tim. Or maybe, he didn't even look very much like Tim at all, and yet, Frank still saw his son in the boy, something he could have become. A version of the life his son didn't get. If he got punished, or maybe even fired, because of him, well, Frank didn't think he could handle that. He had no plan, no way out. He sat there waiting for whatever would happen. The partially eaten tiramisu sat in front of him. Frank dug his fork into all the layers and took a bite too big for his mouth. He wiped cream from his chin and licked it from his fingers. He still didn't care for tiramisu, but he ate every last bite, because he could. Because what else could he do?

Again

It was a record-cold winter the first time Anna died. The frost came early and burrowed into her bones. No broth or fire would warm her. Her blood contained ice, shards in her eyes. Wind gnawed through spaces between windows and doors. The horses' water froze into bucket-shaped blocks. Tree branches, heavy with snow and ice, sagged to the ground.

Anna had been born in a blizzard, back in 1899, to Mr. and Mrs. Pritchard, farmers just down the road from Albert Meachem's family. The midwife hadn't been able to make it to the farm in time in the storm, so her father had had to deliver her. It was a difficult birth; her mother lost a lot of blood. Fortunately, her father had had plenty of practice birthing cows and pigs and was able to save them both. Her mother liked to say she was a snow baby, that cold was in her blood.

It would be three decades before she'd be born again.

In her first life, Albert and the other men cut holes in the ice to fish farther out than usual, over deeper waters crowded with the slow-moving bodies of trout. She fried his catches with what oil she could save. They got by, little by little, but winter took its toll.

Anna made Albert walk across the lake to prove it was solid before she would let him teach their thirteen-year-old daughter Maggie to skate. From the frosted kitchen window, she watched her daughter fall and get back up, carve her blades into the ice and glide. The girl was as stubborn as her mother, as determined. She took to it quickly and all winter, despite the chill, Maggie would strap her skates to her boots and skate whenever she wasn't in school or doing chores. Anna always insisted she wear the hat, scarf, and gloves she'd knit for her. She warned her never to go out without her father.

Albert was the first boy Anna kissed, when she was fifteen and he seventeen, under mistletoe at the Pritchards' annual Christmas party. It was a chaste kiss, a quick peck, but it lit something inside her. While she had always enjoyed seeing him in town, she hadn't really looked at him like that before. She hadn't seen him since the last market day in the fall and he had grown into his body since then, filled out, grown the beginnings of a beard. He was solid in a way that was comforting, a way that she needed. Though the kiss had been circumstantial, a product of tradition, it stayed with both of them. In the spring, Albert began making frequent visits to the Pritchard farm under the guise of trading his mother's honey and pickled vegetables for their milk and lamb. Each visit, he sat with Anna and her mother at their kitchen table, sipping coffee and picking at cookies or bread or whatever she had helped her mother bake that day. Their second kiss was in the barn where no one could see. He held her face in his hands and brushed his lips against hers, as if unsure she wanted to kiss him back.

"Things are getting worse in Europe," he said as they lay amidst the hay. "I've been listening to the radio. German troops are on the move. Thousands of people have been killed already. They've got to be stopped," He gave a long sigh. "I turn eighteen next month. I'm going to enlist." She didn't know what to say so she reached for his hand and they lay in silence until the light faded into dusk.

"Will you marry me when I come back?" he asked, without looking at her. She leaned into his arms and said *yes.*

She feared for both of them; feared he would never return, how it would gut her. She did not yet know that she would see him again in another life, another version of this one. Anna waited for his letters all fall into winter and then spring and dutifully sent her replies to far-away places she'd never visit. She wrote of the news on the farm and in town, trivial things she was sure were far less important than his news, but all she had to offer from her small corner of the world. She worried when his letters stopped coming, but by the next Christmas he was home with a wound that would cause him to limp for the rest of his life, shrapnel permanently embedded in his femur. They married the next summer on his family farm, where they would live, where their daughter would be born, where they would each die. They weathered thirteen winters on the farm together before the coldest one came, the one that would end Anna's life for the first time.

Anna was in the kitchen when it happened, preparing the last of the fall's venison for stew. She was always working; the farm had taught her that. Albert didn't open the door as much as he threw it, bringing a gust of wind and snow in with it, and carrying a drenched and limp Maggie, her wet clothes rimed with frost. He swept the jars of homemade jam and the small vase of dried Queen Anne's lace onto the floor, breaking them all, and laid her on the kitchen table. Albert had been too busy in the barn to accompany Maggie to the lake to go skating. Stubborn as she was, she had gone by herself, in defiance of Anna's admonishments never to do so. Despite the cold, the lake was deep, the ice still thin in spots. It had groaned underneath Maggie's skates, a crack spread, and the frigid water swallowed her. Albert had heard her scream and come running.

Maggie's skin was an eerie blue, ice-cold; she barely breathed. Anna had never been so scared, her normally stoic façade collapsed into hysteria. The only thing she knew to do was take action. She wrapped her daughter in wool blankets and stoked the fire. She commanded Albert to draw a bath to warm her, but Maggie stopped breathing before the water was hot. They buried their only child by the silver maple behind the house, overlooking the lake she loved.

Anna wouldn't last a season without her girl. It was as though her body had internalized her pain, turned it into a burning ache. Loneliness like she had never known. The weight of the loss shut her body down. The fever took her in February. Winter swallowed her whole.

Anna was born again in 1899 to Mr. and Mrs. Pritchard, in the same cabin where she had been raised the first time, a maple tree with a swing in the front yard. The birth was a difficult one and her mother lost a lot of blood. Her father pulled his daughter from her, a wriggling bloody thing. This time, her mother didn't survive.

As she grew, her skin was new again, soft, fresh, no hardened cracks in her hands. Her stomach was taut, muscular, un-rippled by the marks of childbirth. She was both a child and also not, a child with the memory of a mother and wife. She knew too much, had to be careful not to portend the future. She was ahead of her class, carrying the knowledge of a fully grown woman. She missed a daughter who hadn't yet been born. She still carried that burden in her youthful body, a heavy yoke to bear. Her movements were lighter, easier than she remembered. She ran, swam, leapt. Though she moved with more abandon, she lived her second childhood in fear waiting for God to take back the gift he had given her.

If she was good, she thought, if she did everything right this time, she wouldn't be punished again. Everything happened for a reason, she thought, everything was God's divine plan. Her faith stalwart. She believed she could save her daughter by following the rules. Now she went to church dutifully every week and prayed a secret prayer for her future daughter. She said the words, not sure if they had the power she needed, but hoped, hoped for everything.

She saw Albert, the boy she would marry, at church and school and at the annual Fourth of July picnic. He, of course, didn't know what their future would bring. Sometimes, she felt the secret of their future rising to her lips; she knew it was a secret she had to keep. He looked at her like any other girl. He didn't have her memories, of vows and the way he held her in his muscular arms, of those eternal months with him overseas, her not knowing if he was dead or alive. She wanted to tell him what she knew, what would become of them, to take hold of his hand, to curl into his arms, to feel safe. She wanted to tell him to avoid the shot he'd take to the leg in the war, to go with their daughter to the lake. She wanted to tell him everything.

This time, she first kissed him the summer she was fourteen at the edge of the lake. He was bare-chested, having just come out of the river, skin still flecked with water droplets. She and her cousin Susan were picking stinging nettles when Albert and his brothers showed up, laughing and whooping and splashing into the water. She watched the way he jumped into the cold water, the way he swam with precision, his muscled arms making careful strokes, the water parting for him. She couldn't wait. She wanted to see if her past would repeat itself. When she and Susan had filled their baskets, they turned to head home, but Anna told Susan she'd left her handkerchief behind and went back. Only Albert was left, pulling his dungarees up over his wet legs. Without saying anything, she leaned into his lips, lingering there just for a moment. Then she turned around and ran back to Susan before he could respond, leaving him at the lake's edge, wondering what had happened.

Lying in bed that night, she wondered, would that small act change everything? Did it matter if she kissed him in December or July? Would anything change? She assumed they'd get married again, have Maggie again, start over. Though only a child herself, she was still a mother. She couldn't tell anyone what she knew, how she could remember a past version of herself, how history repeated itself.

Her father grumbled as he read the newspaper at breakfast, citing the troubles in Europe. She knew she couldn't tell him what was coming, that she was powerless to stop it, to save the boys and girls who would never return. What good did this strange gift do if she couldn't change anything? The war came again, as she knew it would. Inevitable. Despite her protests, Albert enlisted. Again, she waited, impatient for every letter, any news she could catch on the radio. She imagined the shot that would bore through him, the moment it would strike. She remembered each past letter, everything he told her about his regiment, the long marches and the boredom. She knew the ends of his stories before she read them. Sometimes she got the slightest detail confused with the past; a name that was different or where they fought.

Again, Albert came home, though this time his injured leg had gone gangrene and had to be amputated. They married in the spring at the Meachems' farm. Albert's missing leg kept him from doing much of the farm work and they had to hire a hand to help.

Maggie was again born the year after Albert returned. Despite his disability, he taught her to ride a horse, milk a cow, but Anna warned him not to teach her to skate, no matter how Maggie begged. Of course, she couldn't explain her fear, and Albert believed she was just being overprotective. He would take Maggie to the lake in the first light, while Anna milked the cows and was none the wiser. One morning, she was boiling eggs for breakfast when she caught Albert and Maggie sneaking in the back door, skates in tow. She was furious—hysterical, even—and sat down at the kitchen table and wept.

"How could you?" she asked Albert, much to his confusion. "How could you?"

Maggie tried to comfort her mother, stroking her back and hugging her from behind. "It's just skating, Mama," she insisted. "We didn't do anything bad."

"I know you didn't, baby, I know you didn't," Anna said. "But it's too dangerous. Promise me you'll never go out there again."

"Mama—"

"Anna, don't you think that's a little—"

Anna's sudden sobs drowned out his protests. Albert told Maggie to go upstairs and he sat at the kitchen table and held Anna's hands.

"Anna," he said, "I can't understand what all this fuss is about. Have some sense, woman."

Anna tried to wipe away her tears with her hand. How could she explain something she didn't understand?

"I know this is going to sound crazy," she said, hesitant, "but I've lived through this all before. All of it, growing up, our marriage, dying, everything. And then I woke up again, did it all over again."

"Anna, what are you talking about?" Albert frowned and dropped her hands. "What kind of game are you getting at?"

"I know, I know how it sounds. Just let me—I'm trying to explain. I don't know why. It just happened, I was a woman, same age as I am now, and I died but first she did." She pointed up the stairs. "Maggie." Her voice was getting louder and more frantic. "She died out on that lake and it was your fault! And now it's going to happen again and it's all your fault!" The tears came hot and fast.

Albert stood up and paced the floor, scratching his head, stroking his beard while Anna choked on her sobs and struggled to breathe, phlegm rising in her throat. At last, he spoke.

"Anna, I can't figure a damn thing you're saying. You've obviously gone out of your mind. I'm going to call for the doctor."

"No!" She leapt up and grabbed his arm. "No, please," she begged. "I'm fine, really, it's just a dream. Just a dream, that's all." She leaned into his shoulder and wept.

"Please let me be, please. Don't call the doctor. Please."

But the doctor came and didn't know what to make of her either. She had calmed down somewhat, but still fidgeted, scratching at her arms and fingering her dress folds, constantly moving, buzzing about. She talked too fast and couldn't sit still. Her eyes darted from the doctor to Albert, from Albert to the floor, to the tree out the kitchen window, back to Albert. She couldn't focus on one thing at a time. The doctor called it a nervous episode, gave her a nerve tonic, and told her to rest.

She didn't try to explain her circumstances to Albert again. Instead, she made it her mission to convince him that she was sane and didn't need to be sent away to the place the doctor had mentioned. Things became tense between them. He was always watching her for signs of insanity. Sometimes she'd absentmindedly mention something she shouldn't yet know, like the impending stock market crash and nationwide depression, how they needed to save up, to store enough food. He didn't believe her, didn't understand what she was talking about. He looked at her cautiously, as if he was afraid of her.

One day, Maggie begged to go to the lake, but Albert said it would upset her mother too much, so Maggie snuck out on her own. Again, the ice cracked. Again, Anna had to watch her daughter die on her kitchen table, again lay tulips on her grave under the silver maple out back. Albert didn't say anything about Anna's prediction; it hung heavy in the air between them. He treated her cautiously, like a breakable thing.

This time Anna recovered from her fever and lived through the hard winter. She had been waiting for death to reclaim her, to relieve her from the pain of living without her daughter. It didn't seem fair that Albert had survived a war and she a fever but that Maggie had still died, despite Anna's efforts to keep her off the lake. Why had she gotten to live two lives and her daughter had barely begun hers? She couldn't believe in a god that let such things happen.

This time, she had to endure years of loneliness, the space her daughter left deep in her bones. She lived through the Depression again, then another World War, a world changing around her faster than she could keep up. She and Albert learned to be alone together again. They took care of the farm dutifully, took care of each other, but things changed between them when they lost Maggie. They didn't touch as much. Their conversations were terse and succinct. Anna never said it or even admitted it to herself, but she blamed him for teaching Maggie to skate, for igniting that spark in her that was extinguished. Things were harder between them after that, not that they ever talked about it. She couldn't even bring herself to speak Maggie's name. She felt that she had failed. She'd known what would happen and still couldn't prevent it. Why had she been given a second chance if it did nothing to change the fact of her daughter's death? It was a relief when pneumonia finally took her, a middle-aged woman who had been waiting for death.

Once again, she was born to the Pritchards in a blizzard in 1899. Too much blood, her mother pale and weak, but she made it. Anna realized how much she had missed growing up with her the last time, baking bread together on Sundays, her mother teaching her to do things she already knew how to do. Anna was a survivor, a child of the farm. Cows to milk, pigs and chickens to feed, eggs to collect, land to tend. Again, her parents pulled her from school at thirteen to help on the farm. This time Albert first kissed her on a hayride at the harvest festival the fall she was fourteen.

He brought the Pritchards apples from his family's orchard, which Anna sliced and baked into pies. He made excuses to visit throughout the winter, bringing the Pritchards dried corn and canned preserves. Though he didn't have money to buy a ring, he promised her he'd marry her when he returned from the war. She wanted to warn him about his leg, but was worried he'd think she was insane again, so she kept it to herself. Knowing the future didn't help much if she couldn't change it.

Albert kept his promise and they married on his parents' farm, which they would again inherit. This time, Anna insisted she didn't want to live on the farm by the lake. She couldn't look at that lake or go near it. She begged her husband to move them to the city, as far away as possible, but he couldn't imagine any life other than the one they'd both known. She dreamed of the daughter she knew they'd have. She would keep her as far from the lake as she could. When her father took ill, they moved back to the Pritchard farm to help her mother take care of things. This time, Albert's leg had healed, and he was able to do all the heavy work that needed doing. Albert's brother and his wife moved back from the city to take on the family farm when Anna and Albert couldn't.

Maggie was born on the same day but in a different farmhouse, the same where Anna was born, miles from the lake, where she wouldn't be able to sneak off to skate. Anna kept Maggie close, always had an eye on her. On holidays, they visited what would have been their home, a place Anna remembered as home, though it was no longer hers.

The record-cold winter came again. This time, the fever took hold of Maggie. Anna had warned her not to skate because she feared the lake swallowing her again, but she hadn't considered that winter could get ahold of you in other ways. Maggie was delirious, rambling about the lake and fish and mermaids, making no sense. She was slipping away from herself. Anna's broths and teas couldn't save her daughter.

One night, her face flushed with a hot sick, Maggie's eyes closed and never opened again. It didn't seem to matter what Anna did; Maggie would not survive. Anna wished she could give her daughter her gift, that her girl would wake again and again, renewed. But she didn't know why it happened or how to change it. It didn't seem like what she did made a difference. Whether Albert kissed her in a cart among hay bales and pumpkins or under mistletoe or by the lake, whether his leg returned with him or not, whether they lived on his family's farm or hers, she would still lose her daughter every time. She would have to watch her daughter die over and over, powerless to stop it.

Anna was again forced to live a life without her only child, waiting for death, willing it to be permanent. She was heartbroken to once again be born in 1899 to the Pritchards, to grow up knowing what she would lose. Again and again, she had to watch Maggie die. It was wearing at her. She felt weak, broken, helpless. Her bones were tired. She would rather die, finally, than endure another life outliving her daughter. Whatever strange power she had, it was more punishment than gift. She was forced to wait for death to reunite them.

Wars, inventions, new ways of thinking muddled together, memories overlapping, blurring. Time, a fickle thing. Each new life felt tarnished, a little more muted than the last.

This time, she avoided Albert throughout their childhood and adolescence, hoping it might spare them both pain. Albert didn't kiss her before he deployed. There was no mistletoe, no hay bales or cart, no nettles by the river. He didn't write her letters. He didn't come home. Though she barely knew this version of him, she cried at his funeral, for him, for herself, for the daughter they wouldn't have. She mourned a life unlived.

There were other suitors, boys who came to the farm to buy meat or milk but none she paid much attention to until Clyde accompanied his father to the Pritchard farm to shoe their horses. He was tall and commanding, sure of himself in a way that felt reliable. They didn't talk much that first visit, when Anna served the men coffee and cinnamon buns, but Clyde soon found excuses to come more frequently, bearing gifts of his mother's jars of butter pickles. It wasn't as exciting as when Albert had visited, those clandestine kisses behind the barn, but there was a dependable quality to Clyde and his stalwart dedication to doing things the right way. In the fall, he asked her father for his permission to wed and they were married at the church in town that spring, snow still dotting the mountains.

Clyde's plan was to build a cabin on his parents' property, over the mountain from the Pritchards,' but before they had begun, Anna's father had a heart attack and died alone in the field. Anna and Clyde moved in with her mother on the Pritchard farm while Clyde traveled to his family's farm across town nearly every month to help his father with the horses he bred. He'd stay for a week or more and Anna would be left on the farm on her own. She was despondent; wanted a life different than this but did not seem able to build one. She surrendered, no longer as strong as she had once been.

This time, she had different children than the daughter she'd once known, two boys. Clyde insisted on naming the older one Clyde

Junior. She named the younger one Albert and couldn't explain to her husband why. Clyde Junior was ardently independent, like his mother had been as a child, and would often disappear on one of the horses or to cut trails in the woods. Albert, on the other hand, clung to her. He was her baby. He preferred working with her in the kitchen to doing the chores his father considered "man's work."

Albert loved animals. He'd rather talk to the cows and pigs than to most humans. He even named them all, the livestock, and spent more time hanging around them than playing with the neighbor children. He spent hours in the barn, brushing the horses and tending to them, stroking them and singing to them. He occasionally joined his brother on his long rides through the woods and riverbeds, though he preferred to ride alone, just him and his horse. It made Anna nervous, the boys out on their own, but Clyde insisted boys needed to be outdoors and that she was being overprotective. She was afraid of everything now, knew the dangers that plagued this cruel world.

While Anna loved her sons, she missed her daughter. She missed her rosy cheeks when she came in from the cold, proud of teaching herself to twirl on her skates. Anna missed brushing and braiding her long wavy hair, clipping it atop her head for special occasions. She missed rolling oats and kneading dough with her, teaching her to coax the bread to rise, the rhythm they got into, the way just being near her felt familiar, comfortable, like when she'd done these tasks with her own mother. There was no one she could tell about the hole inside her where her daughter belonged.

She loved Clyde in a different way than she had Albert, but she still ached for Albert's solid arms around her, the scratch of his beard, the way his eyebrow arched when he worked something out. Every once in a while, she called Clyde "Albert" and he assumed she meant their son. The other versions of her life were like shadows looming over her, distorted, a slightly different shape. She privately mourned the husband she hadn't had. She felt that she was losing herself. There was no one with whom she could share her grief.

Her son Albert was thirteen when he and Clyde Junior went horseback riding on a trail through the woods and Clyde Junior taunted his little brother into racing. Albert didn't want to go so fast in the woods, but his brother took off at a canter and he had to follow. He wouldn't live down his brother's teasing if he didn't. He hated when Clyde Junior called him a chicken; he fell for it every time. They raced, whipping past pines and birches and maples, the horses pounding the narrow strip of the path. Clyde Junior pulled further ahead, whooping and waving his fist, taunting his younger brother. Albert hunched down, gripping a fistful of the horse's mane and dug his heels into her side, urging her forward. Her strong legs carried them both over roots and logs, slowly closing the gap between them and Clyde Junior. Then a porcupine lumbered across the trail, spooking Albert's horse. She bucked, throwing Albert from her back and into a large oak. The sound of his body against the tree echoed through the woods.

Albert's horse took off, leaving him on the ground, lying on gnarled roots, out cold. Clyde Junior kept going, proud of himself for beating his little brother so thoroughly, until he saw Albert's horse running alongside his own. He jumped off to grab her reins and walked both horses back to find his brother. When he came to Albert's twisted body, he let go of the horses' reins and ran to his side. There was an angry gash on his forehead, but most of the damage was invisible. Albert was in and out of consciousness. When Clyde Junior tried to lift him, Albert groaned in pain. Not knowing what else to do, Clyde Junior scooped him into his arms and laid him across his horse's back. Carefully, he walked the horses and his brother back to the house, where his mother helped him lift Albert into his bed. His body was limp, weak. His breathing slowed and his face went bone white. Anna held his limp hand all night as he hung on. He was dead by morning.

The pain of losing a child didn't get any easier for Anna. She had thought that this time she could avoid it. She thought it was Maggie who was destined to die, no matter what she did, but Maggie didn't exist in this life and God had to take another child from her. She wondered what she must have done wrong to deserve this, her pain lived over and over, the ache of loving something with your whole being and having it torn away from you. What could she do differently the next time, assuming there was a next time? How could she end it?

Again, she was forced to endure a life after her child's death. This time, she had Clyde Junior and eventually, his two daughters and son, but the losses still weighed heavy on her heart. Clyde's grief over his son's death turned to anger, which boiled in him, dark and hot. His temper grew quick. He never got violent with his wife or remaining son, but he once slammed the door so hard it fell off its hinges and one time, he threw a bowl of stew against the wall, said the beef was tough as an old shoe. Anna grew afraid of him. She shrank into herself. Again, she waited to die.

It was on the tenth anniversary of young Albert's death that she finally did it. While Clyde was chopping wood, she took his rifle from the shed and went up to their bedroom. She sat on a chair in front of the mirror on her dresser and stared in the mirror as if at a stranger, rifle in hand. She did not recognize the desperation in her eyes. She had become a wild thing. If she did this, she thought, maybe she wouldn't come back. She would not lose a child again. She lifted the rifle, the heft of it in her hands, brought it to her temple, and closed her eyes. Clyde startled at the shot.

Again, she was born in 1899 to Mr. and Mrs. Pritchard, who taught her to be useful. Anna met Albert and Clyde in the one-room schoolhouse, though they were both a few years older than her. Albert walked her home from school, two miles out of his way, making himself late for chores and taking his father's belt. Clyde came with his father every time he came to shoe or deliver a new horse. The boys competed for her attention. It was Albert who held her hand, who kissed her on the way home one day when she was fourteen. This time, polio crippled him as a teenager, and he would not be able to fight overseas. This time, she carried her former miscarriages to term and they had three children, a girl, Maggie, and two boys, Albert Junior and Calvin. This time, her boys would skate with Maggie and warn her to avoid the deep part of the lake that never froze all the way through. This time, she would watch her children grow, have their own children, survive.

Finally, she lay in her bed, an old woman with Albert and their children at her bedside, grandchildren in tow. She felt so much older than her eighty years. She had carried so much for so long; endured. She couldn't say how many lives she had lived, how many years—centuries, surely. She was ready.

This Is Not a Drill

We live in Hawaii; are salted and tanned. A farmer, a surfer, a mother. We wake up on a Sunday in January, put on church clothes, comb long hair, then receive a text that says:

"EMERGENCY ALERT: BALLISTIC MISSILE
THREAT INBOUND TO HAWAII.
SEEK IMMEDIATE SHELTER. THIS IS NOT A DRILL."

A little yellow triangle with an exclamation point tells us something bad is happening. Read it again; search for instructions. SEEK IMMEDIATE SHELTER.

Whose name to call first? A husband's, wife's, daughter's, son's? Gather our people, hustle them outside. We need to move, to feel like we're going somewhere. Buckle the kids into their booster seats. Drive. It is any Sunday, sunny, unremarkable. No signs of an incoming missile. Yet.

We live on an island, a place with no bomb shelters, no basements, no way to burrow underground. No ground solid enough to hide under. We live on lava. Our world is burning. Aflame. An expert of some kind estimates that it would take approximately thirty minutes for a nuclear missile sent from North Korea to reach Hawaii. The island where we live is the closest part of the US to Korea, so we will be the first to go. Read the news. We know that the president taunted

North Korea's despotic leader, bragged his big red button was bigger, and now a button has been pressed.

Check the time. How long do we have left?

We live in paradise. Our grandparents were bombed here. They became American. We are American.

Go to the ocean. Gather our babies and hold them tight in the water. Let our hearts slow to the rhythm of the tides; the moon will call the water back, back, back. Our feet cannot touch the sand. Legs kick below. The waters are clear. We are infinitesimal; the ocean is everywhere. How long has it been? How long do we have left? Keep kicking. Look up to the sky. The sun is a missile.

Yes, but.

The thing on the screen looked like an alien or roadkill, a bloody dead thing. The doctor said "ectopic," and Mikayla thought of an ectoskeleton, the way cockroaches wore armor on their backs, and they were practically indestructible. They learned in Bio that cockroaches could survive a nuclear blast, that they had outlived the dinosaurs. Maybe armor wasn't such a bad idea. Although, of course, armor doesn't prevent something from killing you from the inside.

She'd taken health class freshman year but didn't remember much from it. She was pretty sure Mrs. Peters had talked about ectopic pregnancies, which is, she learns, when an embryo attaches somewhere outside the uterus, but Mikayla couldn't have told anyone a thing about them until today. She did, however, remember her prefixes from Latin because the words sounded so good coming from Mr. Gunderson's mouth. *Ecto-* came from the prefix ex-/ect-, meaning *out.* As in *outcast, outsider*, a creature clawing its way *out of* her body.

There was no one to drive her to the hospital. She couldn't ask her mother to borrow the car on a workday; they only had the one now. She definitely couldn't ask her dad to pick her up. Besides, he'd be too busy at work. She'd asked Mel what she was doing first period, but she'd said she had a big exam to take. There was no one else she could ask, so Mikayla walked the mile and a half to the hospital herself. She had thought she was just going in for an ultrasound to explain the bleeding. Now, feeling dazed after all the examinations, the way home was going to take much longer. When the receptionist had asked if she had anyone to drive her home, she'd lied and said yes. Strange that that was the thing that made her cry as she left the hospital; that there was no one to call.

It's late mud season and the entire town smells like dead things. Melting ice and snow has turned the dirt roads soggy. Fallen trees rot. Fields soak up the snowmelt like sponges. Mikayla emerges from the hospital's artificial glow into the overcast spring day. The sky is a bright white light. She wishes she'd remembered sunglasses.

Mikayla has been dizzy for days. All the blood she lost, the doctor explained. The nausea was what made her think she was pregnant in the first place, despite the heavy bleeding for the past week. She is on her way to get pills, ones to end it and ones to relieve her pain. She'll have to call in sick to school tomorrow.

She spent the past week feeling like she had to vomit. That tinny taste filled her mouth all week. The signs were right: nausea, lack of appetite, soreness. The test confirmed it. Two lines equaled yes, one equaled no. It didn't occur to her, or, apparently, the Clear Blue people, that there was a third option: *Yes, but.* As unprepared as she'd been to deal with a pregnancy, she was even less prepared for an unviable one. How do you mourn something you didn't want?

She couldn't tell her mother. Maybe she would have before, back when they used to talk about things like crushes and birth control, when it was all hypothetical. But not now. Over the past year, her mother had confided in her in ways Mikayla wished she hadn't. She didn't want to hear about how oblivious and cruel her father could be. Her mom assumed Mikayla would take her side, but Mikayla just wished there were no sides. She wished she could have stayed with her dad, stayed in their house with the Sharpie notches marking her height in the kitchen. The only home she'd ever lived in, now two miles away and too big with just her father in it.

He got the house; she got the good car and enough for an apartment and the kid. Although at eighteen, Mikayla was hardly a kid anymore. She would graduate in a few months. She still hadn't declared if she'd be going to Amherst or Colby, but wherever she went, she'd be grateful not to be a possession for them to barter with anymore. Her dad had already started holding the fact that he'd be paying her tuition over her mom's head. Mikayla and her dad used to be close, bonding over junk food her mom wouldn't let her have and '80s action movies, but they didn't seem to have much to say to each other anymore.

She'd gone to the doctor after a long, painful period and two positive home pregnancy tests. All they'd determined at that visit was that she had tested positive, definitively, but the doctor warned her, the heavy bleeding wasn't good. They had to take an ultrasound to determine if the fetus was viable. At first the receptionist told her they were scheduling a month out, but Mikayla burst into tears at the thought of not knowing what was in her body for a whole month, and they called her three days later to tell her they could sneak her in first thing in the morning. There wasn't really a chance of good news. Either it was and would soon not be, or already wasn't. She didn't want it anyway, so she didn't expect to feel so sad. She hadn't known she'd leave feeling so empty and lost, with "a ticking time bomb" in her, as the doctor had called the thing in her right fallopian tube.

The pharmacy's fluorescent lighting and neon yellow sale signs are nearly as offensive as the bright beating pulse of the hospital. She feels like throwing up again. Ashley Martinez is working the counter. Ashley isn't the kind of person you want knowing your secrets. Everyone knew that Laura Eldridge had an abortion last year. How did that become public knowledge? If not from Ashley herself, from other Ashleys. Mikayla passes her the scrip without making eye contact.

"Oooh, Vikes," Ashley reads the prescription, smacking her gum. "Have fun."

Ashley goes back to typing and raises an eyebrow as Mikayla steps aside to wait by the condoms. She runs her finger along all the options—ribbed, studded, ultrathin.

"Mikayla?" She turns to see Glory McInnis, her now-former neighbor whose kids she sometimes watches. Mikayla flinches and steps away from the condoms.

Glory has two boys, five and seven, and has always treated Mikayla like the daughter she never had, giving her hand-me-down designer clothes and makeup samples she gets from the department store she works at. And yet, despite these niceties and her constantly insisting that Mikayla can eat *anything* in the house that she wants, Mikayla had always sensed a façade, like Glory really wanted Mikayla to like her, which was off-putting. It was hard to tell exactly how old she was, what with the obvious Botoxed forehead and lips, but she was clearly too young to be Mikayla's mother, and a far cry from her simply dressed, no-nonsense mom.

Glory talks a mile a minute, but Mikayla had barely ever heard her husband speak. Glory always looks like she came straight out of the pages of a Soft Surroundings catalogue, like she's trying too hard to look like a free spirit. "I'm so glad I ran into you; I've been meaning to call. Can you babysit this Saturday? There's this thing Matt and I have to go to, kind of last minute, and your dad said you could use a few extra bucks, since you're going off to college soon…"

Glory is talking too fast. Mikayla feels like she is in slow motion and everything around her is moving with the speed of a hummingbird. She nods along, and suddenly Glory is gone, leaving behind her the scent of fresh flowers, and the vague sense of having agreed to something. Then Ashley calls her name, looks around to make sure no one is in earshot and whispers to her, "If you're looking to unload a few, I know someone who would be happy to take 'em off your hands for a good price."

Mikayla twirls the beads on her bracelet. "Um. No, thanks." She stuffs the bag with the pills into her backpack and continues towards home. It's about a quarter mile faster to go through downtown, but she cuts through the park just a few blocks from her old house. On an overcast April morning the only people in the park are nannies and their charges and a few guys playing basketball. She has to stop in the park restroom to throw up and kneels, her bare knees on the cold cement floor. As she retches, a small child in the stall next to her asks her mother what that sound was. The woman shushes the girl and leads her out of the bathroom, away from the echoes of Mikayla's sickness. There are no paper towels in the dispenser, so she wipes her mouth with toilet paper and straightens her skirt. As she leaves the bathroom, she sees him at the water fountain. She tries to turn the other way before he notices her, but he calls her name and there's nowhere to go.

He plants his hand against the wall above her, closing the space between them, like he used to lean against her locker before he graduated. He says it's been a while with that half-smile that makes her feel noticed. But being seen is the last thing she wants right now. He asks why she's not in school and she shrugs. What is she supposed to say? She wants to tell him that it's all his fault, that he's the reason she has to bear this pain on her own. But what's the point? It won't make it hurt any less. She can't seem to bring herself to say the words out loud, to make it real.

He tells her she looks a little pale and she's embarrassed that he noticed, that she is showing her pain on the outside. She used to like the way he looked at her in the bleachers at basketball games, the way he didn't care if anyone saw him looking. Now she feels exposed, ugly, disgusting. She wishes she could disappear.

"You haven't been answering my texts," he says. The smile has faded from his face.

"Umm…" she starts but doesn't know how what to say. She hasn't written back since the day she took the pregnancy tests. Nothing she could say seemed adequate. "I'm sorry," she says, though she's not sure exactly what she's sorry for. For not telling him, or maybe for letting him touch her in the first place, for everything.

"I see how it is," he says, accusation in his voice. "You didn't even feel the need to break it off, huh? Just ghost me like I'm nothing."

She wants to tell him that it isn't about him, that she doesn't have the words for the broken parts in her.

The tears come on suddenly, before she has time to walk away. She chokes on her sobs and he looks back at his friends waiting on the basketball court, panic on his face.

"Look, I didn't mean to…Can we try this again?" he asks.

"I don't know," she manages to get out through the tears, "I don't know how…" he puts one of his long, sturdy arms around her and she leans into his chest, letting the tears come. He pats her back and tells her it will be OK, that he forgives her. She knows she'll never tell him.

When she and her mother moved out last month, they tried to bring Mr. Mistoffelees with them, but the latch on his kitty carrier broke and he bolted for the woods. Mikayla ran after him, slipped in a muddy patch, and tore her jeans. She came back to the rented U-Haul empty-handed. She hadn't wanted to leave him and convinced her mother to look for him for the better part of an hour, but finally, her mother insisted they go. They had a lot of unpacking to do.

"Cats are extremely territorial," her mother told her on the way to the new apartment. "They don't like to be uprooted."

"Clearly," was all Mikayla had said, staring out the window, watching for Mr. Mistoffelees. Her parents had given him to her for her birthday, when she was obsessed with an old version of *Cats* on Broadway. She'd come back every weekend to look for him with no luck. She imagined his fluffy orange body being ripped apart by fisher cats, coyotes, ermine. Weasels were known for taking the heads off chickens and leaving the bodies.

Mikayla made LOST posters with a picture of Mr. Mistoffelees stretching on his back, showing off his substantial pink belly, tufts of orange fur sticking out from everywhere. The photo made him seem unthreatening. It didn't show his claws or how he always bit her hands when she went to scratch his belly. His eyes were closed in ecstasy; you could tell he was purring.

One day, Glory McInnis had called to say that she had found a decapitated bird on her back porch and did they think it might be from their missing cat? She hadn't called the number on the posters, their new landline, but the old number she had, so Mikayla's dad had to relay the message. He promised Mikayla he'd put out milk in the mornings and would look for Mistoffelees every day after work. He always forgot the *Mr.*, which was the whole point. Her dad had been finding dead things on their front steps and back porch: a mutilated squirrel, a family of moles, half a mouse, but no other signs of the cat.

Ectopic pregnancies are common, the doctor had assured her, as if this fact would offer her some comfort, assuage the guilt she felt at her body creating a life and destroying it, not being capable of nurturing even this tiny thing. If she thought about it, it was the same thing as an abortion, technically speaking. The pills the doctor prescribed her would take only a few hours, she told her, and then it would be gone. She would be alone in her body again. She was almost sure that's what she would have done, anyway. Given the choice, which she wasn't. She wondered if anyone else at school had ever had an alien burrowing its way through their fallopian tubes.

Her mother had told her the story of how Mikayla had almost killed her a thousand times. The emergency C-section, the hemorrhaging, how Mikayla's tiny writhing body had been pulled from her. The blood loss, the pain tearing her body apart, Mikayla's ten perfectly round bloody toes. She wasn't complaining when she told it. She was sharing what they'd gone through together, how they were rooted to each other through pain. And yet, this pain she could not share with her mother. She would not tell her mother that she knew how it felt to be ripped apart.

Mikayla doesn't have to pass the house—her dad's house now—on her way home, could have avoided it, and yet, she stands in front of it as if she were a guest waiting for someone to invite her in. *You don't really notice a place when you live in it*, she thinks. Now she registers its flaws from the outside: the broken living room window that birds were often flying into (her mother had finally put up painter's tape to deter them, so it was now a broken window with blue tape running across it like rivers on a map), the peeling gray paint, a sagging porch step. Her dad hasn't put out the patio furniture or the hammock yet, too early in the season still, so the porch looks empty and uninviting, not the place she used to sit and read, do homework, watch birds.

She feels a sudden desperate need to fall into her old bed. Her dad probably hasn't changed her sheets yet. The room probably still smells like her, despite the absence of all her things. She left her posters up, the bulletin boards with concert and movie ticket stubs and magazine cut-outs that said things like *Dance like no one is watching* and her favorite Toni Morrison quote, "It is always now." She could curl up and be a kid again, pretend her parents were watching TV together downstairs. She was supposed to visit her dad on weekends, but so far, she hadn't stayed over. It felt too strange, like living in a memory, a place that didn't belong to her anymore.

He'd tried to make things like old times, put on *Die Hard*, one of their old favorites, and made ice cream sundaes with M&Ms on top, like they used to have when her mom was busy at library meetings. But it didn't feel the same. She felt like he didn't really want her around anymore. He'd basically disappeared over the last year, left them both, and she was stuck picking up the pieces of her mother that he'd left behind. Not even Alan Rickman's German accent could make it better.

She sticks her key in but realizes the door is unlocked. Strange for the middle of the day. Her dad's always been vigilant about things like that. She feels like a trespasser tiptoeing through the mudroom. Her dad hasn't changed much but the house feels foreign somehow, without her and her mother's things. It smells different. There are dishes next to the sink, mail scattered across the kitchen table, not her mother's usual order. The house she grew up in doesn't belong to her anymore. As she heads up the stairs, she can hear voices coming from her parents' bedroom, her dad's now. A woman laughing. Her father is home in the middle of the day and he's not alone. Mikayla pauses, the stairs creak, and the voices mumble through the door. Through a crack she can see bodies in motion, the pink of their flesh pressed together. She gasps and hears the woman ask, "What was that?" Mikayla holds her breath and tries not to move. She is crouched behind the door when it swings open and slams into her forehead. She stumbles back and hits the wall.

She hears, "Mikayla? Oh my God!"

She blinks and her father comes into focus, in his boxers standing above her.

"What are you doing here? Why aren't you in school?"

"What are *you* doing here?" she fires back, clutching the spot the door hit, where she can already feel a bruise forming. She forces herself up and runs down the stairs, three at a time, before he has a chance to respond. She runs out the door and leaves him standing at the top of the stairs, half-naked, calling after her. She makes it outside and, as she runs, she notices tufts of orange fur on a bloody thing in the street but doesn't stop long enough to examine it. She keeps moving, away from the roadkill, away from her father, away from the SUV in front of the house that she recognizes as Glory McInnis's, away from her childhood, away from the pain.

Rumors

What's left of the old Simpson house is our go-to place to party. The frame is mostly still there, roof gone, floorboards covered in ash and nearly half a century of debris, leaves and signs of generations of partiers—condom wrappers and old beer cans. The stairs lead to nowhere, burned-through about halfway up. We sit on the few sturdy steps and drink warm beer from red Solo cups. There are other places we could go, the river or the woods, but we like to be this close to death. We imagine what it would be like to burn alive. We ask each other how we would want to go. Parker says he wants to be shot, point blank, nice and quick. Shelly wants to drown. She thinks it's romantic and then you don't have to worry about what to do with the body. Kwame wants to go out fighting, guns blazing, action hero style. Tif says she wants to go in her sleep, which is probably the best thing but still sounds super lame. I don't know how I want to die. They come up with plenty of suggestions. We all agree burning is the worst thing we can think of.

Somebody spray-painted a wobbly pentagram on what's left of the wall next to the stairs. Most of us believe that it was done years later by some kids in the '80s who came here to Satan worship, or, more likely, to drink and smoke and fuck and feel tough. Tif thinks whoever set the fire tagged it then, back in '75, spray-painted the wall and that's proof that it wasn't Mr. Simpson or any part of the family who burned it down but some random Satanists causing trouble. She's the only one of us who believes it was an outsider. This is the game we play here, imagining what horrors happened where we sit. It makes us feel powerful, like we can rewrite history.

Everyone in town knows the story. I don't recall who first told it to me or when; it seems like something I've just always known. We told it at sleepovers and campfires, letting our imaginations take over. We still tell it to each other, passing around a joint and speculating on what happened to Emily Simpson half a century ago. It was what drew me to Parker, if I'm being honest, his obsession with death.

What if she comes back? we wonder aloud. *What if Emily Simpson comes home right now and finds us here? What would she say?* We like to have the same debate over and over, whether she too was burned alive, or, like I think, she got away.

The fire was in winter, during a cold snap in early December. Some versions say it was a candle knocked over; some say it was electrical. Parker thinks it was arson and Mr. Simpson himself started it for the insurance claim (they were underwater on the farm's mortgage, they say). Kwame says it was the older brother and that he meant to get out but got trapped. He never meant for anyone to survive, he says.

Mrs. Simpson and three of her four children didn't make it out. By the time the fire department got there it was all gone, the house crumbled, the stench of burnt leather and bone hanging in the frigid air. The barn still stood, cows going crazy. They actually busted through the wall on the hot side closest to the house. Now the barn is collapsed, just a pile of wood. Mr. Simpson survived, left with smoke in his lungs. He sold the cows and the land and bought himself a trailer, planted it on the far side of town, by the river. He kept to himself after that.

The oldest daughter, Emily, was never found. She was fifteen at the time. The charred bones of Mrs. Simpson, her seventeen-year-old son, and her six-year-old twins were recovered, burnt and horrible, but no sign of Emily. There are stories of her showing up years later, coming back to the family farm long after her father had died. He never stopped looking for her, dedicated his life to following the rumors of her living. With these kinds of stories, it's impossible to tell what's true.

Parker and I first had sex on a blanket on the dirty floor of the only room that still has walls on all sides, which I imagine was Emily's room. I found a slightly melted locket on the floor afterwards and pocketed it. It's too charred to see whose pictures are in it but I pretend it was a gift from Emily's lover.

Shelly says the whole thing was set up by Emily's secret boyfriend, that he burned down their house so he and Emily could get away. Her theory is she got pregnant and had to flee. But she insists that Emily didn't know what he was going to do, how her siblings would die trapped in their rooms. She prefers to think Emily wasn't the kind of person who could do a thing like that.

I think she did it. I think she conspired to burn her house down with her family inside. I don't know if she wanted them to suffer, to die, or if she just wanted to escape. I prefer to think of her as someone who just wanted love. I like the boyfriend theory. I think that could be right, but the boyfriend in my version wasn't some creep who manipulated her and killed her family without her knowing. I think she talked him into it. I think she was so wildly in love that she was consumed by her need for him; she just wanted to be with him all the time, so close she could crawl into his skin. They started talking late at night, under the stars in the back of his pick-up or on a blanket in a corn field, about what it would be like, just the two of them. He asked her to run away with him. *We can go anywhere,* he might have said. *Yes,* I imagine she said, *yes.* But it wasn't that simple. Her parents would never let her go. They'd make her finish school, stay home to take care of her younger siblings, make sure the cows and dogs and chickens were fed, that the table was set, that everything was as it should be. Besides, they didn't approve of her boyfriend. Who knows why? They didn't want him taking their daughter away.

I imagine Emily and her boyfriend asking her parents for their blessing. Young Emily and her lover holding hands hidden in the folds of her dress, sewn by her mother. That Emily set the table and her mother laid out fried chicken, coleslaw, pickles, and still-warm oat bread. They sat around the table and Emily coughed, then told her parents they were planning on getting married and leaving. This would not do.

Emily's plan, I imagine, made her parents even angrier than mine were the time I stayed out all night with Parker without texting them. I remember being stubborn and defiant, certain that our love was more important than my parents' rules, bigger and wilder than anything. I imagine Emily's love was like that, a hot thing, a flame, burning her up. I think we could have been friends, Emily and me. I don't tell anyone this. They all talk about her like a tragic figure; they think she was the victim. But I can see being blinded by love. I don't want them to know that I can understand a thing like that.

Family Portrait

Idabelle had been dead a week by the time the family photograph was taken. Ma wanted it done sooner, while her body still looked like *Ida*, but the photographer got delayed by the storm. We had to wait six days past when he was supposed to come to town for the Easter festival. It was a grand affair, having a photographer come to town for the first time ever. Most townspeople likely couldn't afford to have their photograph taken, but many had been saving up, waiting for the chance.

The festival was postponed because half the town was snowed in. I don't remember snow ever being that heavy in April before, but Pa says that's cause I'm too little, and back in 1869, when I was just a baby, it snowed so much in early May that he couldn't plant corn until the beginning of June on account of the ground being froze.

We'd never had a family portrait taken. None of us had ever had our photographs done, except for Pa, during the war. His whole regiment sat for a photograph together. It's printed and framed in the living room. My older sister Pamela wanted to have a photograph of herself taken at the county fair. Pa told her that a photograph just for the sake of having a photograph is too great an expense.

"Then how come there's one with you in it?" she asked, later that evening.

"That's different." He ran his fingers over the dusty glass of the image of him as a young solider next to other soldiers whose names I do not know. It's the only photograph in the house. There's no proof of the rest of us. I read in school that some cultures think a photograph captures your soul, as if it were a concrete thing that could go missing, be trapped in sepia forever. Maybe Pamela wants to be trapped, to live forever.

When Ida was taken by consumption, Ma insisted we have a photograph taken of all of us together, so she could remember all of her children. We couldn't bury Ida until the photographer could come from Boston. And so, we had to put her in the root cellar. My brothers, Richard and Paul, wrapped her body in blankets and carried her down the steps. She stayed there for nearly a week, next to the turnips and potatoes, wrapped and perfectly preserved at four years old.

Ida was the youngest of the five of us; she took over for me as the baby. I remember when she was born, even though I was only five at the time. The midwife came from across town and Pamela, the eldest, took us kids to play outside while my mother howled. When we came back in after hours of playing in the woods, a slippery little thing was crying in Ma's arms, and they called her Idabelle.

The day after she died, I went down cellar when no one was paying me any mind. I sat with Idabelle, pretending we were playing Ring-Around-the-Rosie, playing sleep, playing dead.

Richard and Paul were always annoyed at Ida tagging along, slowing them down, at all her incessant questions, but I adored her and treated her like my real-life baby doll. I liked braiding her hair in elaborate plaits, playing Pat-a-Cake and House with her. Pamela insisted she was too old for such silly games, so it was usually just Ida and me.

Ida's sickness came on quickly; her skin went flush and hot. We weren't allowed in the room with her, in case we got sick, too. It was only a matter of hours before Pa walked out of the room, shaking his head in defeat. Ma wouldn't leave Ida's side.

Once the photographer finally arrived, I helped Ma and Pamela make Ida look alive again. Pamela did not want to touch the dead body, but Ma insisted we help. She did not say much as she painted her youngest's cold face, trying to bring her back to life in appearance at least, rouging her ghost-pale cheeks. Pamela used a stick of coal to smudge her blue eyes, make them look alive again. I tied her favorite yellow ribbon in her curly blond hair. She always asked me to do her hair like mine.

We had to prop her up against Pa's trunk and Richard and I were stuck holding her shoulders to keep her in place. Her body was cold from the cellar and stiff as wood, half-frozen.

The photograph sits on the mantelpiece beside the photo of Pa and his fellow soldiers, all of us together. You almost can't tell that Ida isn't as alive as the rest of us, except for the eyes, vacant and looking far-off, as if she has a secret.

Chopped

Since Mike, our youngest, went away to college, Derek and I have been eating a lot of meals in front of the TV, or, specifically, while watching *Chopped*, which seems to always be on the Food Network. We've started to eat dinner in front of it most nights, not sure what to say to each other. We need something to fill the silence. I don't know what to say to him if we're not discussing carpooling or who's going to which game or performance or weekend sleepover plans.

I've never considered myself much of a cook—nothing special, anyway. I made meals the kids liked; homemade mac 'n cheese, lasagna, hamburgers and roasted potatoes. But now that they're both in college and thousands of miles away—they both insisted on getting as far away as they could—Derek and I have been eating a lot of premade and frozen meals. It's different with half as much food to make. I keep buying more than we need and having to throw out rotten apples and potatoes with eyes. I have to halve recipes. Single servings just make it easier. Sometimes I buy things out of habit, like beef jerky or Double-Stuf Oreos—Mike's favorite—and they go uneaten for months. But Lean Cuisine meals aren't bad, mushroom-stuffed chicken in a white wine sauce, beef tip stir fry, pesto tortellini.

After work, Derek and I change from our pressed suits into jeans or sweats, hit the couch with a bottle of wine, and tune into the Food Network and there it is, like always; dependable, safe. We listen to each of the four competitors' stories and we both pick who we think is going to win the $10,000. Then, in each of the three heats—appetizer, entrée, dessert, all made with four mystery basket ingredients—we make bets on who will be chopped when one person is selected to be eliminated at the end of each round. The unlucky contestant is revealed after a commercial break by presenting that person's dish under a cloche that host Ted Allen (of *Queer Eye* fame) picks up, and everyone gasps. Loser of our bet has to do the dishes or take out the trash. It gives us something to hope for.

We like it when the chefs screw up, burn the meat or forget the sauce with three of the four basket ingredients in it, especially when more than one person screws up in a round and we and the judges have to decide which is worse, forgetting an ingredient or undercooking the meat (usually the most significant offense). Derek always sides with the cockiest competitor who brags about how much better he is (it's always a "he") than his competition. I prefer the humble ones, like the single mother of three with bright pink hair, who make sure to commend everyone in that awkward period of time where they have to talk together in front of the camera while they await the judge's decision. There's clearly a cue card they get with possible responses: "It could really be any of us," "I think it's a toss-up," "That was harder than I thought it would be," or "Good luck."

Everything is quieter without any kids around. It's just been Mike these past two years, since Amy went away to school. It's not like he was that rowdy or anything by himself, but there was a noise to his presence, his clomping around the house, slamming the fridge door every few minutes. His friends arriving like locusts tearing through the house after practice. There was a rhythm to him that's been disrupted and the quiet sits with us. I had hoped things would be better between us once Mike was gone, less restrained, maybe, but so far that hasn't been the case. I don't know who I am if not a mother and wife.

It's been nearly a year since I found out about Derek's affair with Tina, a woman from his office with hair that always looks like she just stuck her finger in an electrical socket. I've seen her at the company Christmas parties and the occasional retirement party over the years.

I always found her a bit abrasive, even before. She was usually drunk and talked too loudly. She'd do things like put her arm around me and ask me to go to the bathroom with her, like we were friends. She quit shortly after I found a Facebook message with a photo of her bare breasts when Derek was still signed into my computer. Derek assured me it was over. He claimed it wasn't really about her, that it was about *us*, that something was missing between us. Of course, I had felt it too, but hadn't wanted to admit it, hoped it would resolve itself, like things usually seem to over time. I don't know how to start over, how to redefine myself, build a new life. And so I stay, keep things the way they've always been, at least on the outside.

Derek has to go to a conference across the country, so I'm left alone for a few days. Alone with my thoughts, my doubts. I text Amy but it always takes her days to respond to me. She must be too busy living her own life at college. We used to be close but now she has a new life without me. It's the way it should be.

The first night on my own I eat a bowl of cereal for dinner in front of the TV. While I watch chefs whip up beef tongue and ricotta gnocchi with chard and pancetta, I slurp gray milk from my bowl of Raisin Bran. I don't know what to do with myself on my own. What did I used to think about, before worrying about report cards and permission slips and PTO meetings? Who am I if not catering to everyone else's needs? Who will take care of mine?

I log onto Facebook and see Derek's profile picture in the corner: he's logged in on my computer, again. I know I shouldn't, but I look in his messages and there she is, just a few days ago. "See U @ 7 tmrw. Can't wait. xoxox." That was the night before he left.

Tonight, it's an amateur chef episode, which are my favorites. They mess up the most. Instead of every tiny error being fatal, there are egregious errors all over the place and it's harder to guess who's going to get chopped. One girl burns butter and tosses the contents of the flaming pan into the garbage, which sets the bin on fire, and she watches in disbelief as the flames eat the trash can. A man in jeans and a black t-shirt has to put the fire out while the chef waits, helpless. I feel like that sometimes.

On my last night alone, I decide to cook. I need a purpose, a distraction. I'm going to compete alongside the *Chopped* chefs. Of course, I won't have the random and obscure ingredients they have to use. I'll have to make do with what we have in our fridge and pantry, which will be enough of a challenge, I think. In the twenty-minute appetizer round, the chefs on TV have to use octopus, maraschino cherries, won ton wrappers, and endives. I find a nearly-full jar of maraschino cherries in the door of the fridge (when did we buy these? And why?), half a cabbage that has browned and gone a little soft. Nothing resembling octopus, so I chop up a frozen fish stick. I tear up tortillas and fold them into won ton shapes with the fish, diced cabbage, onion, and garlic, and fry them while I boil down the cherries and mix them with soy sauce and diced ginger. It takes me twenty-two minutes (too long) and I eat them as the judges taste the dishes in front of them, pretending they're eating my dish and complimenting my creativity, though the execution, I'll admit, leaves room for improvement. The breading has fallen off the fish and gone soggy. The cherry glaze is sickly-sweet, but overall, it's not a bad dish. I think I'd go on to the next round.

One man tells the audience that he'll use his winnings to visit his mother in Haiti, whom he hasn't seen in over a decade. He'll give the rest of the money to her, he says. A single mother tells us all how she'll be able to turn her life around with $10,000, get her own place, how it will save her. I try to think of what I would say I'd use the money for. In reality, I'd use it to help pay Mike's tuition (Amy's on scholarship) this semester and it would still only barely make a dent. But that doesn't sound very exciting, so I think I'd say I'd go on a cruise around the world.

I wanted to kick Derek out when I found out, but I worried about Mike. In reality, he probably would have been fine. He was already seventeen by then. I think I was making an excuse to myself. I was scared, scared of the unknown. Derek slept on the couch for a few days, then came back to our bed and we pretended everything was fine. We're pretty good at it.

For the entrée round the chefs have to use fried chicken, mint chutney, rock candy, and sea beans (what are sea beans?). I take frozen green beans, frozen chicken fingers left over from Mike—he loves those things—green curry paste, and candied ginger I find in the pantry that's gotten a little hard. I peel the breading off the chicken, coat it in the curry, and bake it. I fry the green beans and toss in the ginger to coat them. The chicken comes out a little dry. The green beans taste better than they look. The plate looks a little bland, somewhat sickly. Another failure. I don't think I'd move on to the dessert round, except for one of the chefs forgets to plate the sea beans and is, predictably, chopped. She talks about how disappointed in herself she is. I know how she feels.

The single mother gets chopped for overcooking her chicken, like me, and for not transforming the basket enough. She tries to hold back tears while telling the camera what a talented group her competition was.

The Haitian man makes it to the final round, along with a young guy hoping to use the winnings to buy an engagement ring. I'm rooting for the Haitian. I want him to reunite with his mother. I wish they'd show the happy afterwards scenes.

The ingredients are coffee, white chocolate chips, mint liqueur, and Nilla wafer cookies. My guy's making coffee ice cream with chocolate chips. I love when they make ice cream; they screw it up at least half the time, too runny or over-churned. His is perfect. I'm making Grasshopper pie with slightly-freezer burned mint chocolate chip ice cream instead of the liqueur. It's a safe bet, no-bake pie. I might be chopped for my lack of creativity. I try not to think about what to say to Derek when he gets home. We're going to have to confront this, however much I want to ignore it. But I can't afford to get distracted now; I'm on the clock. While the pie sets in the freezer, I whip up heavy cream, like everything I know, everything I have, depends on it. I stir and stir and stir.

Love Lines

I have three lovers and let them love me the ways they know how, with knuckles and tongues. One runs her finger along the crease of my inner thigh; another kisses my neck softly, a whisper on skin; the other's knuckles crawl up my spinal column, slow and hard. I have three lovers and none of them knows my hunger, how their kisses will never fill it, how I long for hands and mouths and soft parts. What I have done for love. I have three lovers and mix up their names, their birthmarks, their tattoos. I have three lovers who tell me they love me and I don't tell them I know that's a lie. I say thank you and mean it. I am a selfish person. Never enough. A Narcissist, one of them says more than once. Not enough empathy, another says. I have three lovers and none of them knows me. *What does it even mean to know a person? What does it mean to know yourself?* People fall in love with me and fall out of it. Words are just words. I have three lovers and I will leave them all.

No One Will Ever Hear You

I was waiting for the walk signal on my way to work this morning when a car passed and I heard it, the scream. The car wasn't particularly noteworthy—old beige sedan, nothing fancy. The driver didn't strike me either—average middle-aged white man, brown hair. What I noticed was the scream coming from the car's back window, a child's high-pitched desperate siren of a scream. This wasn't a regular tantrum-on-the-way-to-school scream. It was the same desperate, glass-shattering scream I spent six years perfecting, praying someone would hear me, save me, even though I knew God couldn't hear me any more than the neighbors could. This child's scream sounded like that: a life-depending-on-it, bloody-murder kind of scream. I closed my eyes, trying to fight going back to that place in my head.

The trouble is, unless you've had as much practice and time to study screams as I have, it's hard to tell the difference, especially with kids. Most people shrug their screams off as petulant and annoying, which is exactly what everyone else on the street corner did. Some looked up for a second when they heard the kid wailing out the car window but quickly looked back at their phones and coffee cups. The child—a girl, I think, though I couldn't be sure; the hair was relatively short and she, or maybe he, couldn't have been more than five—threw themself desperately against the tiny back window. I swear, my heart stopped for a second. I was that child, panicked hands leaving sweat marks on the back window. Only when the man who serviced our furnace took me when I was eleven, I rode in the trunk. No one heard my screams.

Even though I'd been anxious about being late to work for the second time this week, when that car passed and the light changed, I stood rooted to the sidewalk, unable to move for several seconds. While people who'd been next to me crossed, I stared as the beige sedan disappeared around the corner and the child's persistent scream faded.

In that moment I was back in a basement cell where I hadn't been in eleven years, when I was seventeen and an electrical fire finally caught someone's attention. I could feel the rusted chain around my ankles again, the damp underground air that smelled like my own blood. The scream was my own, too, wild and panicked, ricocheting off cold cement walls.

I screamed until my head felt like it was going to explode, my throat raw and dry. I screamed as loud and hungry as I could. I screamed as often as I could, whenever I heard the upstairs door slam and then felt the frame of the rotting old house shake. I'd count to one hundred and wait until after I heard the tires crunch over the gravel and pull away down the street.

Even though it didn't help, I screamed and screamed, imagining a nice family walking by, or maybe neighbors who would hear me and call the cops. I didn't know there were no neighbors. He'd blindfolded me and brought me in in the dark. I hadn't seen the sun in years. I hadn't seen another person. I had barely spoken, only screamed. I had to believe someone would recognize panic in my scream and come for me. But no one heard. Or they couldn't tell I was anything but a child pitching a fit. Either way, no one came.

The first time he found me screaming, I braced myself, expecting punishment. But he just laughed his horrible laugh. "Go on," he urged in his low, gravelly voice. "Scream your little heart out. No one will ever hear you." And I believed him. I believed that I would never get out of that basement. I stopped fighting him. I let him touch me. I went to a place inside myself where I knew no one would hear me.

I shook myself out of the memory and found myself running, not towards work, but in the direction the beige sedan had gone. I didn't even decide to do it; my feet just started to move. Maybe I'd see something, I thought, as I darted between casual walkers, almost tripping over a dog's leash. A license plate number, some detail reported on an Amber alert, *something*. Maybe I'd be that savior that had never come for me. Or at least, not for six years. This child could be on her way to a basement cell, too.

I didn't have time to think how ridiculous I was being, how I had no reason to believe this random child was in danger, how I had no way of knowing or doing anything about it. How, even if I took the time to go to the police, they'd laugh at me for reporting a kid screaming in a moving car. I ran towards the car as it disappeared over a hill. I ran, even when my heel snapped and my ankle rolled. I ran towards myself in a cold basement in the middle of nowhere. *I'm coming*, I thought. *I hear you.*

Buy Her Flowers!

No one was there when my mother fell. She lay in her own blood, out cold, at the bottom of the wooden stairs for hours until the cleaning lady showed up the next morning. There was bleeding on her brain, a broken jaw and wrist, dislocated hip, angry bruises everywhere. She lives alone. She's only sixty-eight.

I missed the call on my drive to work and didn't listen to the doctor's message until I got there. Despite having not talked to her in almost a year, I was her emergency contact, the only family member within three hundred miles. I was still in my car when I heard the message, in the office's parking lot, and I just turned around immediately. I took a week off but constantly had to answer emails from the hospital waiting room. I had to go back to work and now I visit first thing in the morning, I visit on my lunch break, and again after work. I get a slice of pizza and a Caesar salad from the cafeteria, which isn't all that bad, and eat dinner with my mom, who pokes at her salmon and eats a few overcooked green beans. Lately she's been refusing the hospital food then complaining they never fed her. I've been bringing in chocolate bars and Ritz crackers with peanut butter to up her calorie intake. I get her chocolate milk from the cafeteria but it sits untouched until I drink it, and by then it's warm.

After I'd tried to kill myself last year, I landed myself in a psych ward. Even though it was only a twenty-minute ride on the T, my mother didn't visit me once. Never answered my phone calls from the hospital. My brother Robby admitted she'd told him not to tell anyone where I was, that it was obvious she was ashamed. She didn't seem to understand that blaming someone for their mental health issues could send them into a spiral of shame and guilt. At least, that's what it did for me. It was like I was sixteen and manic all over again, with her telling me to snap out of it, calm down, talk slower, get it together, when I knew what she meant was "don't be yourself."

This is the third time I've visited her today. It's been two weeks and she's out of the ICU and in a rehab facility, which she insists is doing her no good. There's more light here, I try to convince her, those east-facing windows. These doctors are good, I say, they're high-rated. She's not buying it. *I'm trapped here*, she keeps saying, *trapped.*

Her room is filled with vases of flowers, a rainbow of flowers on every surface in the room, some on the floor so you have to watch where you're stepping. The flowers keep coming, big ostentatious arrangements from family, friends, former co-workers. To be honest, the smell has gotten a bit cloying.

Mom is convinced the nurses are stealing her flowers, just like they're stealing the chocolate bars I've been bringing her. Never mind when I point out the wrappers in the trashcan; she still won't believe she ate them. She swears the nurses took the leftover mac 'n cheese I brought last week, which she doesn't remember eating. Every time I visit, she insists I take home vases of flowers. My apartment is now filled with the sickly-sweet smell of rotting roses, Gerber daisies, and phlox. They're on the kitchen countertop, the desk, the coffee table, the TV stand. I'm running out of room.

At first, the hardest thing was not knowing how or if she would improve, if she'd walk again, feed herself, be able to write her name. She would be able to do all of those things and many more. Then the hardest part became arguing reality with someone who could not remember eating breakfast. *They took my flowers again*, she laments, and she gets angry when I remind her that she made me take two vases this morning.

Being in her hospital room reminds me of my own room at the Twin Pines Psychiatric Unit. I had a desk, which was nailed to the floor, and my bed was perhaps slightly more comfortable than a hospital bed, but it looked basically the same. Same persistent glow from the fluorescent lights in the hallway. The feeling of always being watched.

It's atrocious, the way they're treating her in here, Mom says. I try to remind her that they're treating her well, she just forgets, but having the same conversation over and over is getting old. At least she knows where she is now, knows she doesn't want to be here, and is getting most of the basic questions right: where, when, how. When she was still in the ICU, she answered, *We're in Paris, we are at a concert*, or, *I'm here for a meeting*. Or, most often, *I don't know. It is 2005. It is last year. It is March. It is summer. It is snowing.*

She doesn't know that Mother's Day is this weekend, doesn't know it is spring and her daffodils are coming up without her. Everywhere I look, there are Mother's Day sales, cards, chocolates, gifts that will all be useless for my mom. All this cheap, worthless crap to tell your mother what she means to you.

Robby says he'll visit but it's almost a month before he makes it. "I've been so swamped," he explained, as if that's a reason to leave your mentally unstable sister to handle your overbearing mother alone.

Darren and his wife, Alyssa, flew in a few days after her fall, when Mom was still in the ICU, still bruised on the collarbone, shoulder, hips, the stitches on her jaw still raw and red, when everything was still uncertain. *Brains are unpredictable*, the doctors had explained, *there's so much we don't know*. They visited her a few times but went to the cafeteria when doctors came to speak to her. I was in there every minute I could be, documenting and remembering for her. I will say that Alyssa helped by cooking dinner every night they were here. I'd been surviving on take-out from the Chinese spot down the block. Moo goo gai pan and egg rolls, General Tso's chicken and pork fried rice.

On their last night in town, through a mouthful of Alyssa's mushroom risotto, Darren said, "So, I've been thinking, and I think what makes the most sense is to sell the house and have Mom move in with you."

I take my time swallowing my bite, trying to compose what I'd say to him. The truth was, that thought had occurred to me, but I'd been trying to avoid it, delay the only clear choice.

"We can't afford to pay her mortgage and our own, and I know you can't on your salary. And you know she won't want to move halfway across the country to live with us. Robby can barely take care of himself."

"She needs full-time care," Alyssa said.

"Why does it have to be me?" I asked. No one answered.

On the way home from the hospital, my passenger seat is filled with flowers, sloshing their pungent water in their ceramic vases. I must have twenty vases now, nowhere to put them. The seatbelt sign tells me that my passenger is insecure. A sign outside a flower shop says *Mother's Day Is Coming—Is Your Mother Special? Buy Her Flowers!*

Mini Van

Blue-gray Dodge Caravan, 1999. It was my mother's but she bought herself a Subaru and gave her old van to me, told me it was my turn to drag my sisters to ballet and lacrosse practices. That's how I became the first of my friends to have a car, everybody's designated driver. There's a marker in the back that can write on windows and people are always drawing dumb shit on them, mostly dicks. The van's got big bench seats that can fit seven people in seatbelts, but we can squeeze three or four more in the back and between the seats. On this night it's just the four of us, though, Jenny and Todd and me and Jason. We're on our way home from a party where we didn't know anybody besides each other. Some girl Todd knew had invited him, but we didn't even see her there. I'm not even sure whose party it was. Isn't it always that way?

Whoever's house it had been lived way out in the boonies in Sutton, the town next to ours, the Gold Town, as everybody in Pittsdale calls it. Just next door but nothing like Pittsdale at all. It's just as small as Pittsdale, but it's where rich New Yorkers and Bostonians own second homes or stay in the Chi-Chi hotels and go to the spa. Everybody walking around in their leather boots and high heels looks like they belong in *The OC*. They have boutiques and bistros; we have the burger barn and Walmart. But still, our football team almost always beats theirs. Go Seahorses.

Jason was the quarterback for Pittsdale for two years. He got thrown from the championship game his senior year in the third quarter for starting a fight with a guy who clocked him from behind. He still hasn't forgotten it; on the way to the party he said, "I hope that asshole's there so I can show him a thing or two."

The house we were at was nice but not Sutton nice. They were probably considered poor in Sutton for just having a normal, nice-ish house, no bowling alleys or movie theaters or things like I've heard some kids in Sutton have. We've been to a few parties there and usually everyone's playing beer pong in a room full of antiques and expensive furniture, not even caring when they spill, doing Jell-o shots in kitchens with marble islands. This one wasn't like that. This was a place I could actually see living in. Plastic-covered couches and one of those shuttered windows that opens into the kitchen.

We're moving our way through all the people when I hear someone mumble "Pittsdale motherfuckers." Jason hears it too. He goes up to a guy who's laughing and punches him in the face. Next thing I know there's a lot of yelling and Jason is pushed out the front door and me and Jenny go after him and Jenny spills her beer on me and no one knows where the hell Todd is. Jason's still yelling about rich bitches when we get him in the car. Todd acts all fishy when we find him in the passenger seat. I'm pretty sure he was snorting something on my center console. It looks sticky with white residue.

So here we are back in my mini-van, circling around back roads through Sutton, Jenny smoking cigarettes in the back, not even out the window but right into the car and how am I ever going to get that smell out?

It's Jason who comes up with the idea. No surprise there. He's always coming up with stupid stuff to do. A few weeks ago, he took one of the baseball helmets from the gym, put it on and climbed on top of this guy's Jeep, held onto the rack while the guy did donuts in a muddy field 'til he tossed him. I'm sorry to say I witnessed the whole spectacle and when he finally was thrown, I ran over to see if he was hurt or what. He was laughing, clutching his ribs and howling hysterically. Two of them turned out to be broken. He thought that was even funnier.

Anyway, Jason said it and everyone else went along with it, convincing ourselves it was a good idea to burn Sutton's team sign. It's this big billboard over their field with the Rebels' mascot, which, confusingly, looks like a Revolutionary soldier. It's got the triangle hat and everything. There was a whole big deal about the mascot this year, a petition to ditch the rebel because of the inference to Confederate soldiers in the Civil War, which seems kind of like celebrating slavery. The petition didn't get enough signatures.

So, Jason wanted to burn the thing and none of us protested. I think we didn't really believe he'd do it, at least that's what I'm telling myself.

"Fuck 'em!" Jason said.

"Fuck 'em!" we all said.

I have no particular vendetta against Sutton, but it feels so good to have something to fight against. Todd cranks up the music, some loud bass-y dubstep he and Jason are always listening to that I can't understand.

As we get into town, I'm careful to go the speed limit and come slowly to the only stop sign. The streets are empty this time of night, nothing around here open, not even a gas station. We don't pass any other cars. I could stop the car. I could refuse to drive onto the field, whooping and waving my arms out of the window. I could stop him, but I don't.

Jason rips the cardboard box of PBRs from the back seat and lights it. He marches right up to the sign and holds the flaming cardboard to its base. It takes a minute to light, but once it does, the whole thing goes up quickly, the rebel disappearing into flames. We watch it burn.

Relief

They had been walking in silence for the better part of an hour, slowly making their way up the old logging trail behind their house, their Aussie darting in between trees ahead of them, no doubt chasing squirrels. The path was uneven, puddles and ruts. At one point, Ella stumbled and slipped in the mud, scraped her knee. Ryder helped her up. She thanked him and pulled her hand back. They didn't know how to touch anymore. Hesitant, as if afraid of hurting each other.

The first signs of frost showed in the wilted ferns and white-tipped grass. Branches were bare now, the last signs of foliage fallen away, leaves scattered on the ground, rotting. Stick season, they called it here.

They followed the dog up the trail, first Ryder, then, a few steps behind, Ella, always following his lead. At a crest in the hill, where it flattened out into a field, they stopped for water and noticed a graveyard.

"There must have been a road coming through here, back in the day," Ryder said. "Maybe people even lived up here. Farmed or whatever."

"It'd be pretty hard to farm up here," Ella said, "This looks like pretty much the only flat spot."

"You know what I mean." He spat and handed her the water bottle. *Why did they only bring one water bottle?*

She took a swig, handed it back, and went to inspect the gravestones. They looked old, a century at least, crumbling and askew, some of the etchings hard to read. She found one that had cracked down the middle, as if a bolt of lightning had struck it to emphasize the damnation of its poor inhabitant's soul. The dates had disappeared in the crack, but the name was still legible as Dr. Henry Thorton. She traced the letters, surprised by the cold of the stone. Reverend Paul O'Brien's stone had a marble angel sitting atop it. Mrs. Nathan Adams was a "loving wife and mother." No first name. The largest headstone belonged to Mayor Jonathan Peterson, a big obelisk looming over the other stones. How would Ella and Ryder be buried? Another thing they didn't talk about.

Ryder paced between the gravestones, examining the damage. "Look how sunken this one is," he said, pointing to one that had sunk into the earth at a heavy slant. It said "Mary, Wife Of." The name was underground.

"Mary? That's all she gets?" Ella knelt in the dirt, staining her jeans, running her hands along the stone, too, bumpier than the other, thinner, more fragile.

"What do you mean?"

"She didn't even get an identity, just like she belonged to him. No one even remembers her name." Ryder had nothing to say.

Ella began digging with her hands. She scooped grass and dirt from the base of the stone, frantic, digging for this forgotten woman's name.

Ryder sighed, as if debating whether to stop her.

"Ella…," he began, uncertain. "What are you doing?"

She paused, sat back on her heels, wiped her dirty hands on her jeans and began again.

"Her whole identity is wrapped up in him. Even now, his name is literally sinking into her decomposing body, still in control over her." Tears stung her cheeks but she didn't wipe them away, didn't stop digging.

He squatted beside her, placed his hand on her shoulder, saying nothing. There was nothing to be said.

She paused at his touch, glanced at a tiny grave nearby, only a few inches tall, no bigger than a brick, that said only, "Baby Boy."

She and Ryder's baby didn't get a grave, no body to bury, not even a feeble acknowledgement like this one. Nowhere to put their grief. There was no gravestone over which to mourn, nowhere to place flowers and trace a name on stone. They hadn't settled on a name, though they had a list. She believed it would be a girl, though they hadn't wanted to know. Privately, she'd been thinking of her as Isabel, her grandmother's name.

"Oh, Ella," he said, his tone soft. He put his arm around her shoulders, pulling her into him. She leaned against him. It was the first time they had touched in a while. Too long.

"Tell me what to do. How I can make it better."

"There is no better," she said. "This is what we get."

When the blood came, she knew she would lose the baby. She could feel it in her body. Anxiety wracked her body, heartbeat too fast, and she was afraid that it was hurting the fetus, that she would make it worse with her worry. There was nothing she could do; she had never felt so powerless. Ryder tried to convince her it would be alright, reminding her that the doctor they kept paging on weekends when the bleeding got worse had said this was normal, nothing to worry about. But she knew. They'd already told people, too excited to keep it to themselves. It made it that much worse, having to revise the news. Ryder had pulled away from her since then. Their conversations became safe, schedules and to-dos and what to eat for dinner. So much unsaid.

Ryder gently guided her up to standing, away from Mary's remains. How would Ella be remembered; wife? Mother?

They walked through the rows of stones, Ryder's arm around Ella, the dog trotting behind them.

"Look at that one," Ryder pointed to a small, simple stone with only one word on it, no dates.

It said only RELIEF. But whose?

Death Shift

Tanya breathes into her gloved hands, each breath a puff of smoke suspended in the cold air. The bus is six minutes late. The snow's coming down hard now. She shuffles from side to side to keep herself warm. Her winter parka was in her room when the fire started, where everything burned, the synthetic material melted, so she's wearing a thin windbreaker and two wool sweaters. She feels bulky and cold. Her purse is heavy with a ham-and-cheese sandwich and Mr. Katonis's morphine. She checks her phone again, but the time hasn't changed. She doesn't want to give his uptight wife the satisfaction of having a reason to let her go. Mrs. Katonis has already fired two of the other nurses. She told Megan that she didn't clean the windows well enough (not her job, as it said in their contracts). She claimed Debra ate her food without asking. Ashlee had been chastised for taking too many breaks. According to Ashlee, the woman had it out for her.

"We're not her maids, for Chrissakes," Ashlee had complained to Tanya last time they were both at the office picking up paychecks. Besides the briefing during shift changes, this was the only time they had to talk to each other and Ashlee tended to let it all out.

"She's exactly the type of rich bitch around here who doesn't care about anybody but herself," Ashlee continued. They sat in two of the three chairs in the office, beside their boss' rolling chair at her desk. It was just them and the administrative assistant, who was ignoring them while writing emails and returning phone calls.

"Mmm-hmm," was all Tanya had to offer.

"I mean, doesn't she realize how understaffed we are already," Ashlee had asked, "without firing half our staff?"

"I doubt she's thought about that," Tanya said. Ashlee was right; Mrs. Katonis is the kind of woman so wrapped up in her own private tragedies that she doesn't think much of others' struggles. Tanya had dealt with plenty of this type, wealthy white women who think the world revolves around them. *Rich bitches is right*, Tanya thinks.

"I just know she's gonna fire me for some stupid reason," Ashlee continues. "Who knows? She won't like the smell of my lunch or something. Then it'll just be you and Sandy trading shifts there, and I'll be down a job."

"You'll be fine," Tanya assured her, though she wasn't sure this was true.

The bus finally arrives. She is the only passenger. It drops her off at the bottom of the hill, a half mile from the house, which doesn't seem so bad when it's above zero but today feels impossibly far. She trudges up the icy hill in her traction-less Payless boots and slips, scattering the contents of her purse and banging her right knee on the ice, hard. She swears, gathers her things, and keeps walking. That's one thing she's learned: how to keep moving.

Tanya always gets the death shifts. The other nurses say it's a curse. Even though Tanya doesn't pray or believe in that kind of thing, she thinks that if curses were real, she'd be the kind of person to be cursed. Of course, it's not pure coincidence, how many deaths she's seen and cleaned up after. As a home hospice nurse, death is literally part of her job description. But still, most patients seem to hang on when the others are working. It's a game of Russian Roulette that they play, who's going to get the death shift. They even place bets on it, when it's going to happen, gambling lunches or the best shifts.

She arrives at the door in a cold sweat and Mrs. Katonis admonishes her for being late, as if her busy schedule is inconvenienced. Tanya knows the woman doesn't work, if she ever did.

"I expected you ten minutes ago," she says in a clipped tone.

Tanya doesn't bother arguing that his condition seems unchanged and she didn't miss much. She can feel her knee swell under her jeans and long underwear. It'll leave a good bruise.

None of them want to be there for this one. It was always a bit awkward, having to counsel the survivors, being the one to get done what needed doing. No one wanted to play that role for Mrs. Katonis. She had a perpetually severe look on her made-up face. Tanya always had the feeling she was pretending to be younger than she was; she must have been in her seventies but her taut, rubbery skin suggested Botox. Her high cheekbones made her look even more intense.

They'd been waiting for weeks for Mr. Katonis to go. After every shift, they placed their bets, but he'd still be there the next time. With every day he hangs on, the stakes of their bets get higher.

"This one's all you," Sandy whispers as she hands Tanya the chart. "It's gonna happen today for sure. And Saturday's my daughter's birthday," she adds, a not-so-subtle reminder that she could use a shift off. Of course, they all could. They work 24-hour shifts and have to stay at the ready the whole time. Even when patients sleep through the night, they get no real sleep.

Tanya didn't even take a day off after her house caught fire. There wasn't much she could do, anyway, the volunteer fire department still putting out the flames, too much smoke. Her twenty-one-year-old son Brian, who still lived at home, had to stay at a friend's while she and her husband cleaned up late into the night and went to work the next morning, as usual. The fire department determined that it was electrical, originating from a faulty connection in the Christmas lights she'd strung over the windows. She was in the kitchen when it happened. She smelled plastic burning and saw smoke, gathered the cat and dog—*thank God*—and ran outside without her coat. Her son and husband were both at work. She stood alone waiting for the fire department, surrounded by her animals.

Mr. Katonis doesn't seem much different than he did during her last shift here, three days ago. Perhaps his collarbone is more pronounced, chest more concave, cheeks sallower. His skin has darkened to the color of dusk, blood vessels swollen and dark purple veins like the blue lines of rivers on the maps he keeps on the shelves. A few months ago, when he was in better shape, he'd shown her the maps. He'd been a Naval Officer, which she knew from the photos of him in his uniform on the mantelpiece. He still looked like himself in the black-and-white portrait. He couldn't remember whether he'd eaten breakfast or where he was, but he could recall battles with precision and recounted them for her while tracing the routes on his nautical maps.

Mrs. Katonis hands Tanya a cup of coffee and a saucer of cream and asks if she has the morphine, reminds her it's almost time to re-up his dose, before she's even taken her coat off. Tanya takes off her gloves and digs through her purse. Her fingers find her sandwich, Chapstick, her leather wallet, a hairband, hand sanitizer, a crumpled receipt. No morphine. She'd picked it up at the pharmacy on her way, which made her have to take two different buses. She keeps digging, as if it will materialize, but she knows where it is: in the snow where she slipped. She could walk the half mile down the icy road again to try to find it, though it might already be buried in snow by now.

When she admits her mistake, Mrs. Katonis's lips purse in a tight line. The silence hangs between them until she finally says, "I knew you were incompetent. You call tell that agency that you won't be coming back here. We need someone who can actually do their job."

Tanya tries to tell her she can go back and get it, but the woman's having none of it. It seems like she was just waiting for an excuse. They had engaged in awkward small talk, but her tone had always seemed pinched, cold. Just like a dozen other wealthy women Tanya had worked for, women who thought that their money made them important. Women who had never worked a day in their lives, unlike Tanya and her mother before her, always expected to do someone else's dirty work. Tanya wanted to tell her to shove it, but what was the point? She wasn't going to change this woman's mind.

Before Tanya has time to call her husband to come get her so she doesn't have to make her way down the treacherous road and wait for the bus again, she sees Mr. Katonis clutch his chest, shaking. His breaths are shallow and rattling, a sure sign. They both rush to him.

It doesn't take long. Mrs. Katonis holds his limp hand, bony since he's lost so much weight. The rattling stops; he goes silent. Her face softens just a bit. No one says anything.

Since Tanya has been here, the past few months, she hasn't seen them touch. In fact, Mrs. Katonis rarely comes closer to him than the kitchen across the room. But, in this moment, there is a tenderness between them and Tanya almost feels bad for the woman, about to lose her partner of half a century. Tanya goes into the next room (there are so many rooms in this house!) to give them some space. His wife sits with him until his chest stops heaving, the rattling breaths quiet, his face goes dark. Tanya lingers in the kitchen to give them a moment. She scrubs a coffee ring from the countertop to keep her hands busy.

"Do you have children?" Mrs. Katonis asks, her voice cutting through the silence and across the room, wavering.

"Yes, two."

"They take everything you've got." She lets out a sound that is almost a laugh, clipped and precise. "Don't get me wrong, we live for them, don't we?" Her tone has shifted into comfortable territory, as if they were old friends. "But they change you. I was a different person before them. So was he. We were in love once, you know."

Tanya doesn't know what to say to this. She wants to leave but feels obligated to wait until things are settled. Despite this woman, she's not one to shirk her duties. Her mother, a nurse herself, always used to say, "A job worth doing is a job worth doing well."

Tanya walks to where Mrs. Katonis sits beside her husband's body and crouches next to her. The woman has softened. It's if her chest has been ripped open and Tanya can see her raw, beating heart. She's come undone.

"They do change us, but I think they make us better," Tanya says, with sympathy. She suddenly wants to hug her husband, her children, to tell them how much she loves them. To live with no regrets. Mrs. Katonis looks at her and Tanya notices the tears welling in her eyes, her mascara beginning to run.

"I'd like to think so," Mrs. Katonis says, quietly. She doesn't let go of his hand. "He was a wonderful father," she says.

Tanya thinks of reaching out to her, putting a hand on her back, comforting her in some way, but decides against it. Mrs. Katonis doesn't seem like the touchy-feely kind. After a minute, Tanya turns away to give her space to mourn.

"I'm sorry," she says. She has a vision of herself sitting at her own husband's bedside, years from now, holding his hand, remembering their life together.

Mrs. Katonis seems to have forgotten she told Tanya to leave. She stays with the shell of her husband while Tanya moves around her. There are things to be done. Tanya has the routine down by now, four deaths in the last month alone. She logs the time of death, calls the funeral home to come get the body, calls her agency, changes his diaper for the last time, puts the trash in the bin in the garage.

Tanya is no stranger to physical labor. After the fire, she filled contractor-sized trash bags with burned clothes, wood, and debris. She swept up ash, scrubbed walls and floors, sprayed Febreze everywhere, but the smell of smoke still clung to the curtains and furniture. Her efforts felt futile. Their home had been destroyed. Sometimes, Tanya's entire life felt futile—the long hours, so much time spent away from her family, tending to other families' pain. Putting so much love into the wrong places.

The Katonis' adult children arrive one-by-one, too late, shedding layers of coats and scarves onto the bench in the mudroom. The oldest daughter arrives first, somber and serious, then the son comes with a woman Tanya hasn't met, with two blonde kids trailing behind them, and finally, the younger daughter rushes in and asks a slew of questions: *When did it happen, How did he go, Did he say anything, Who was here, When's the funeral, Where's the will?* There's always someone like this, someone in a frenzy making the death urgent.

Someone orders pizza and no one asks Tanya if she wants any. They gather in the living room (or is it the family room? Or the den? Tanya doesn't know the difference). Someone digs up a bottle of wine and they reminisce loudly, as if the volume has been turned up. No one seems to hear the doorbell ring, so Tanya answers the door. The delivery guy hands her the pizzas and the older daughter comes over to pay. He looks over her shoulder and asks, "Is that a dead body?" She turns to look at her father, as if noticing him for the first time, and says, "Yes. Yes, it is." As if that's a normal part of his delivery route.

Tanya calls her husband to come get her, whispering into the phone so as not to disturb the Katonises.

In the other room, laughter, loud voices, sighs. Another bottle of wine. They have a cellar full of expensive-looking bottles that she noticed when putting his sheets in the laundry. Tanya spent Christmas with this family instead of her own, even though Ali was home from school and Brian and her husband off work for the day. Usually, they chopped down a tree and put it upstairs in the loft so its lights shined brightly over the snow from the large window behind it. But the fire three weeks before Christmas took out most of the top floor, which still smelled like ash. All her clothes were gone. She got what she could from Goodwill and her co-workers brought in extra sweaters and home-knit socks. Plastic sheets sealed off the upstairs, where the kids' bedrooms were. Brian moved into the basement. Ali was sleeping on the couch while she was home. This year, the tree was smaller and went on the first floor. Mrs. Katonis gave Tanya cookies for Christmas and she thanked her. As if cookies were what she needed most. Ginger and sugar cookies with green and red icing shaped like snowflakes and fir trees and stars. They were too perfect to be homemade.

It was lucky she was there, Tanya tells everyone about the fire. She saved the dog and cat and the whole bottom floor. It would all be up in smoke if she hadn't been there. If she hadn't traded shifts with Ashlee so Ashlee could go on a date, they'd have lost everything. The frame of the house is still there, only the top floor charred. Tanya the Savior, the Keeper of the Home, the one everybody could rely on who never showed her cracks. A bit like the stoic Mrs. Katonis, whose family seemed to look to her for the answers.

Mrs. Katonis emerges from the room with her children and sees Tanya sitting on the couch, scrolling on her phone, waiting for her husband. Mrs. Katonis sits on the couch beside her and says, "I'm glad you were here when it happened," her usual sharpness gone from her voice. Her eyes seem bluer with tears pooling in them and Tanya notices the resemblance between this refined older woman and the young bride smiling with her new husband's sturdy arm around in the photograph next to his Navy portrait. They look happy in their formal garb.

Tanya agrees; she knows how to handle an emergency, whereas people like Mrs. Katonis tend to crumble under the pressure. It's about knowing how to take care of yourself as well as everybody else, Tanya thinks, as she waits for her husband to take her back to their home, to what remains.

Pen Pals

It was the closest thing to a relationship she'd had in a long time. They'd never claimed to be dating, of course. It wasn't like they could go on dates. But she had someone's attention, which she hadn't even realized how deeply she'd needed. She'd had one relationship she could call serious, though they broke up after she wanted to move in together and it became clear his future plans didn't include her. She'd tried dating apps but had only gotten a few dates and they were so depressing that she deleted her profiles. One guy was at least a decade older than he'd said and all he could talk about was his dead wife. Another asked her if she was ready for kids before they'd even gotten their main courses.

When she started writing to him—just something to do, really—she hadn't really expected their letters to go anywhere. Maybe part of what made her feel safe writing them was that there was no future, none that seemed real, anyway. She read about him in the local paper. They called him a modern-day Robin Hood. He'd embezzled from the Fortune 500 company where he'd worked and gave—or redistributed, as he said on the stand, which she'd watched on TV—the money to union organizers, socialist organizations, the food shelf. Of course, he got tax kickbacks for these charitable gifts. But he insisted in his testimony that he did it not for personal financial gain but for economic justice.

The papers made him sound like a villain, but on TV, she saw another side of him. He was well-spoken and, even in the orange jumpsuit, he looked distinguished, serious, someone she might want to talk to. Besides, his crimes hadn't really hurt anyone besides a big corporation, which was uber-rich, so that wasn't so bad, really.

The first time she wrote to him she told him she didn't blame him, that it seemed to her that his were victimless crimes and that she respected his convictions, his generosity. She once stole a fancy lace bra from Victoria's Secret, she confessed, and was too afraid to even wear it. At least he did something meaningful with what he took. She hadn't expected him to write back.

His handwriting was small and neat, much more precise than her own rushed linked letters.

Did she ever wonder, he wanted to know, if her actions, her day-to-day decisions, really made a difference in the context of the world, or was she one of those people who believed that whatever she did, things would balance out in the end and whether she went right or left, had regular coffee or decaf, whether she bought the store brand or the local one, didn't ultimately matter? That is, he wrote, did she believe in free will or was everything they did predetermined? Did deviating from the expectations of society really do anything, or were the results already planned?

She had never really thought about it before, whether if she went to work on time or she stayed home in bed all day had any impact on the world whatsoever. But she didn't want to sound shallow so she wrote that actions mattered but there was always the possibility of redemption for their sins, the errors they made along the way, and, thinking on it, perhaps there was a greater scheme for them both, some destination they were not yet privy to that they would reach, regardless of their transgressions. Perhaps, he wrote back, the transgressions themselves were what brought them to the predetermined end result. That is, he wanted to believe that his mistakes, that his current situation, were part of a path that would bring him to where he was meant to be, and that her writing to him was a part of that plan, too. He needed to believe in that, she could see; she knew he needed her to believe it, too.

He asked her what she saw on the outside, who sat on the bus beside her, how the coffee and bagel she bought once a week tasted, whether she ever switched up her order or if she always got extra scallion cream cheese, what songs she heard on the radio. She started paying more attention so she could report back every detail to him. She wrote to him about her African Fat-tailed Gecko, Beetlejuice, how he inhaled whole live crickets, how he flicked his tongue at her. She wrote every detail of what she cooked and how she made it. She liked the way it made her feel important, as if her observations of the minutiae in her life, which TV shows she binged, which fantasy novel she read, what she had for dinner, mattered to someone. She imagined it was like what sharing a life felt like, someone to whom to recount the details of her day so she could make the day feel less meaningless.

He didn't tell her about what went on in the prison, what his days were like, except for what he read, everything he could get his hands on—a mix of philosophy, history, and thrillers, which sometimes had pages torn out so you would never know the ending. His letters were often peppered with quotes from *The Communist Manifesto*, which was the only book he owned. He kept it under his pillow to protect it. She bought a copy at a used bookstore so she would know what he was talking about. To her disappointment, she didn't understand most of it.

After a few months of exchanging letters, he asked her to visit. It was a two-hour bus ride, then she'd have to go through security and be searched, a prospect she didn't look forward to. She didn't like being touched by strangers. She didn't respond for a week and he sent her another letter, this time saying he *had* to meet her and please come. He had nothing to look forward to but her visit, he wrote. She complied. The day she was getting ready to make the trip to the prison she changed three times before deciding on a simple but sophisticated cardigan and khakis, the most wholesome thing she could find. She hoped she looked straightforward and trustworthy, steady, put-together.

He looked smaller in person than he had on the news, less imposing, even frail. The lines on his face were more pronounced up close—chiseled, one might call them, deep and precise indentations like erosions on a rock face. He had aged since the snapshot they ran on the news, his peppered dark hair graying, making him look older than his forty-six years.

When they sat down across from each other, his eyes settled on her neck and she thought he must be looking at the freckles that dotted it like constellations until he said, "Those pearls make you look like an elitist greed-monger," his tone accusatory and cold. She fingered the pearls on her neck. "They're fake," she said in a small voice. She thought he didn't hear her but then he said, "Even worse. Ingenuine and self-serving. You want to look like you belong to a class you don't. You idolize wealth, you worship it. Just like the rest of this country." His tone was one of disgust. The way he looked at her made her shrink into herself.

"I don't…" she looked down at her hands. "I don't…" she didn't know where the thought was going. He was right. She wanted to be something she wasn't. She'd thought the pearls would impress him, would make her look like someone he could trust, someone he wanted to touch. She felt like her greed and foolishness were on display, like everyone in the visiting room was staring at her, judging her like he was judging her.

His demeanor shifted and he calmed, his voice softened. He spoke as if he were performing a speech in front of an audience of one.

"'They have nothing of their own to secure and fortify,'" he recited, "'Their mission is to destroy all previous securities for, and instances of, individual property.' You see?" He reached out his bony hand to hold hers and a guard warned that there was no touching. "You have to let go of possessions and greed so we can be together. We could save the world."

And she almost believed him.

When You Are Not Home

Ari sits on the swing her dad hung in the backyard when they moved into this house, when she was in first grade. She remembers holding the wooden posts steady while her dad hammered nails into the beam to secure them. Now the swing is loose and wobbly and the wood is rotting. Besides, she is too big for swings, almost thirteen. The old wood groans with each drag of her legs in the dirt. The swing sways unevenly to the right, then left, in over-exaggerated arcs. She bides her time until it is safe to go back in and watch TV.

Her mom's speech is muffled and distorted, but Ari catches a few words through the closed kitchen windows. If she arches her neck and leans the swing way to the right, she can see them inside, her parents' anger-dance through the house, words shouted from the far end of the double-wide. Despite being unable to hear most of it, Ari gets the gist well enough. It's a familiar argument; the same one her parents have been having for as long as she can remember. Her dad's perpetual joblessness and inability to pay child support. Her mother's 'neediness and control.' She thought that at least the yelling would stop once her dad moved out. But whenever he shows up, they resume as if nothing has changed. With the baby on the way and her mom's boyfriend Joe making minimum wage at the garage, things are tight, Ari knows. They've been eating a lot of canned things.

Ari tried to grab the school copy of *The Giver* as she ran out of the house—she has to read a chapter by tomorrow—but she couldn't find it. She could have sworn it was on the floor next to her bed.

Things have been going missing lately: her mother's cast-iron pan, a can opener, silverware, a hammer, now her book.

The voices are getting louder now. She hears more familiar words like *liar*, *bitch*, *slut*. She twists the swing around and lets it slowly unwind while she spins erratically and watches flashes of her parents in the kitchen. The world is going by very fast now. Fast and blurry. Flashes of her mom, the swell of her stomach like a half shell, then trees, grass, sky, Mom. Dad reaching out to her. Tree, sky, one yellow bird floating above her, Mom stumbling back. Ari wants to stop there and turn back, and she drags her flip-flops in the dirt. The swing pulls back in the opposite direction and brings her with it. She digs her heels in and turns back to face the window, where she sees the blur of a hand swiping through air out of her periphery and hears the loud thwack of skin on skin. Somehow it hurts more now that he's supposed to be gone, and she doesn't want to be near them anymore. Her mother is screaming now, pointing outside.

The door to the trailer opens and her dad backs out slowly while swears and accusations follow him. He turns and makes eye contact with Ari, just for a moment. They haven't spoken more than a few words since he left.

"Hey, kiddo," he says from across the patch of grass that counts for a lawn.

"I said *get out of here*!" Ari's mother yells from inside.

Her father turns and says, "I'm just talking to my daughter," and Ari scrambles to get up. She can't listen anymore. She's sick of being stuck between them. She jumps off the swing, into the air and feels like she'll fall to the ground but doesn't. She catches herself and stumbles into a run.

"Ari!" her dad calls from the doorway.

She runs to the woods behind the house. She spent a lot of time in these woods when she was younger. Dad promised he'd build a tree house back here when they first moved in, after the swing set, but he never did.

She keeps running until her lungs feel like they're going to explode. She's never been very athletic, always the slowest one in her gym class. Finally, she slows and walks. She looks behind her, even though she knows no one is coming. Ari keeps moving through the woods until she is sure that, even if anyone does come looking for her, they wouldn't bother going this far.

She hasn't been this far back here in years, in fact, hasn't even gone beyond the edge of the woods since she and Kelly used to play hide and seek back here. Ever since Kelly started dating Brendan and doesn't have time for her anymore, Ari hasn't felt like playing all the stupid baby games they used to play. They're older—she is older—now. Besides, the woods are different alone. She used to like coming out here, where you couldn't see past the trees on any side. It felt magical then. Now it's kind of lonely.

It's not quiet, though. Serene, maybe, but not quiet. The woods are alive with noise, birdsong and squirrels chittering, branches cracking and leaves shuffling, the soft sounds of wildlife mostly hidden from her. She feels that she is trespassing against something, some secret that doesn't belong to her.

Ari figures she'll just wait somewhere out here until her parents are gone and she doesn't have to hear them yelling. She just wants to be alone. There was a place, she remembers, where she and Kelly used to come when they were eight, nine, ten. It was kind of like a natural fort, two fallen trees that crossed over each other and leaned against a third, a giant maple, forming a triangle between them that was the perfect size for two young girls, even Ari, who the other kids called fat. She was taller now, more average-size, still kind of chubby in the cheeks, she thinks. She bets she could probably still fit. She wonders what it looks like now, if the trees have rotted. If the dreamcatchers she and Kelly made three summers ago still hang on a branch of the lowest tree.

She hears the crunch of branches near her, as if someone has stepped on them.

"Hello?" she asks, too quiet for anyone to hear.

No answer. She spins around, searching for a clue or direction, but everything pretty much looks the same, trees everywhere, mostly indistinguishable. She closes her eyes and remembers the way they used to come here after school. When she opens her eyes again, the spot is straight ahead; she swears it. She walks past almost-familiar trees, mossy rocks, through swampy ferns and past an open clearing freckled with wildflowers where she and Kelly used to race. Kelly always won.

She keeps walking, though her feet are muddy and wet by now, leaves and grass stuck all over them. She bends down to pick up a piece of bark or something off her ankle. It is too soft and she brings it up to her face to inspect it. It's paper, a small strip torn out of a book, from the look of it. It's just a few lines, half gone, caked in dirt so that only every few words are visible.

Strange, she thinks. Why would this be out here? Did anyone else come to the woods behind her house? Maybe it wasn't hers as much as she thought. She wasn't sure where to go from here, and besides, the trees she and Kelly used to play in were probably rotted and fallen apart by now. She crumples the scrap of paper into her jeans pocket and heads back the way she came.

The sun is low and emitting bright pinks, oranges, and purples. The air is getting heavy and cold. The sun has been gradually setting earlier as fall creeps up the east coast. It goes down around seven or eight now, Ari figures. When darkness swallows the woods and everything around her begins to look shadowy and blurred at the edges, she walks home. She knows her mom leaves for work at six-thirty on the dot and it has to be well past that now. Her mother works the night shift at the 7-Eleven and says that the turnpike always takes forever this time of night.

The door is unlocked, as usual. Not much to steal, Ari figures. Without all her dad's tools and miscellaneous stereos and radios and junk, the place seems pretty empty. Joe hadn't brought much with him when he moved in, just a few outfits and a Bible, from what Ari had seen. Besides, he and her mom have been making room for the baby. It's all about the baby now. It's not even here yet and she already feels like it's taking over their lives, taking her mother away from her.

She tiptoes into the house, even though she knows no one is home. Her mom must be at work by now, and Joe would be out, doing whatever it is he does. He doesn't like to stick around much when her mom isn't there, which is fine with Ari. She wonders whether that will change once the baby comes and kind of hopes it won't.

All the lights are out and a dusky haze filters through the windows. It's an eerie time—in-between light and dark, past day but not quite nighttime. She shouldn't be here. She should be at the soup kitchen where she normally volunteers on Sunday nights. But her mom usually gives her a ride on her way to work, and she's long gone by now, for sure. Ari figures they probably wouldn't even miss her at the soup kitchen, anyway. There are always plenty of people on Sunday nights. Good Christians go to church on Sunday mornings and decide to get their good deeds done for the week that evening between football games. She just needs community service hours. Forty a year is mandatory for school. Last year she cleaned cages at the animal shelter but developed allergies and had to get a doctor's note to stop.

She doesn't feel like being around anyone right now, anyway. She just wants to flop down onto her bed and sleep for the rest of her life. And definitely not talk to her pregnant and moody mother, or Joe, or her dad. As she comes into the living room—which is basically just an old couch and a small TV on top of a crate full of random magazines, clothes and wrappers scattered all over the dirt-brown carpet—she can tell something is off. She can feel a strange presence in the house. It's like when you know someone is watching you. She doesn't see any signs of anything strange, but she knows someone is in the house.

She walks slowly, as quietly as she can. Halfway down the hall, just past her mom's open door, she hears noises coming from her room. Something falling. She hesitates for a moment and even considers hiding in her mother's closet until whoever it is goes away, but something in her makes her legs move toward the noises in her room.

The door is open; that she notices right away. She always keeps it closed, in case her mom or Joe decides to snoop around. She doesn't want anyone looking at her stuff. Especially not her journal with all her drawings. It is her most precious possession and for a strange moment she is worried that someone stole it. *Why would anyone sneak into our house when we're not home to steal my journal?* Just thinking it makes her feel like an idiot. Her light is on, which is also wrong. She always, *always* turns it off, even just to go to the bathroom down the hall or to get something from the kitchen. She wouldn't have left it on, not even when she ran out of the house when her dad showed up.

She tiptoes toward her door as quietly as possible, the muddy flip-flops she still has on sinking slowly into the carpet. She is afraid to breathe. She stops at the doorway. There could be a murderer in her room. There could be anything in there. She taps the door with one finger and pushes it open with a squeaky whine.

Cold air engulfs her. The only window in her room is wide open and the curtains her mother sewed from old sheets flap in the breeze. She catches a glimpse of movement outside the window, and sees the silhouette of a man, big and ageless, and then he is gone. For just a second, she can see into the yellows of his eyes, but then it is only darkness.

Someone has been in her house, in her room. Someone strange and unwelcome. Ari doesn't know what to do first. She could call the cops, but she would have to answer a million questions that she doesn't have the answers for. Besides, he's gone now, so what's the point? Unless he wasn't alone. She scans her room. She crouches on the stained carpet and peeks under the bed. Nothing but dust balls and hair ties. She runs over to the closet and throws the doors open. Just clothes, mainly from Good Will and the Salvation Army.

She could call her mom, even though she knows she won't pick up when she's working. There's a number for the 7-Eleven held up on the fridge by a magnet shaped like a tooth with some dentist's phone number on it. She's never called the store before, but she could, and tell her mother—what, that someone was in her room so come home right away to protect her? Her pregnant mother working the night shift. She couldn't do anything to protect her. It would only freak her out, calling her now. Besides, she has no desire to speak with her mother at the moment.

Ari combs through all her things methodically, cataloguing each item she finds in her journal. She pulls all of her jewelry—mostly cheap plastic and colorful beads—out of her jewelry box, just to make sure it's still there, because she can't think of what else a thief would take. She looks through the drawers in her nightstand and desk, normally stacked high with books and magazines. Everything in the drawers seems normal enough, not that she remembers half the stuff in there anyway; it's where she keeps all her junk: old cards, crumpled photos of her and her parents when she was younger, one half of the broken heart "Best Friends Forever" necklace she and Kelly bought together in fourth grade, safety pins, gel pens, Melon Lip Smacker and old purple nail polish that's gotten all gunked-up and dark in spots. Nothing special. But as she puts all this stuff back into her desk drawer, she realizes that something is different. Her desk is neater. The pile of books usually scattered across the surface, taking up all the room to do homework on, is much smaller than normal.

She's run out of space on her small bookshelf for all the books she reads, so they tend to stack up on her desk until she brings them back to school, or the library, or wherever she got them, except for the ones she takes from the laundromat's Take-One-Leave-One box. She's usually the one doing the laundry these days, so she's been in there more often, but sometimes she goes just to scope out the books and slip one into her backpack if there's anything good. There are no other books in the house.

Everything she's read this year had been on that desk, but now there was only a thin pile of a few *Seventeen* magazines she'd swiped from the doctor's office and a copy of Anne Frank's diary that she'd read for Social Studies and wrote a book report on last year. She should have returned the book by the end of the school year but evidently had not.

The Giver is definitely not on her nightstand or her floor, where she swears she left it last night before falling asleep. And she knows that her big fat *Complete Sherlock Holmes* that her grandma gave her for Christmas was on top of the way-too-small pile on her desk. And *The Island* and *The Telltale Heart* should be there for sure. Had that guy stolen her books? Why would someone break into a crappy trailer like theirs and steal her books? They weren't even fancy or anything, paperbacks, except for the Sherlock Holmes, which was leather-bound and old-looking, her grandmother's from when she was young. The rest of them were ripped or had cracked spines and had been probably read by lots of people before her.

Nothing else seems to be missing. The kitchen seems normal, small and filled with a tower of dirty dishes in the sink. There isn't really anything to take in the living room, besides old furniture and a plain lamp. The TV is heavy and old and has not been moved. They don't have a DVD player, just a VCR, but they don't even own any VHS tapes anymore. She doesn't want to go into Mom and Joe's room and probably wouldn't know if anything was missing in there anyway, so she goes into the only other room— the bathroom. The cabinet above the sink is wide open. Pill bottles and tablets without boxes or labels and loose Q-tips are littered around the counter and sink, a tube of Neosporin with the cap left off.

A box of gauze lies open and empty on the countertop. *Why would a thief take Neosporin and gauze?* Ari wonders. As the thought comes to her, she notices red spots like constellations on the bathroom tile. *Because he needed it,* she realizes.

She walks back down the hall into her room. She hesitates for a moment at the door, then marches in, pretending not to be afraid. That's when she sees the red smear on her windowsill. She leans over and inspects it, a few inches long, bright red at the edges, like a cartoon flame trailing a jet engine, and a purple-black glob in the center. Blood.

"An injured man broke into our house and stole gauze and books," she says out loud.

She sits on the edge of her bed but is restless and stands up again. She could call the police. She could say she saw someone climbing out of her window, he left a trail of blood; maybe they could find out who he was that way. But it might be too late. He could be really hurt. Wouldn't he go to a hospital then? Maybe not, if he couldn't even get gauze without stealing it from a random person's house. It seems like he doesn't want to be found. She heard on the news one time that there was a burglar around who stole random household items, tools and kitchenware and stuff. More of a nuisance than a criminal. Is that why things have been going missing? The man had faded into the darkness before she got a good look at him, but she saw a flash of his eyes. They were begging her.

She could wait until the morning, but it might be too late. Ari grabs a flashlight from the junk drawer in the kitchen, and checks the batteries, which she's surprised to see work. She steps into the early night. Darkness is still settling in around the edges of the evening. She's not sure what she's looking for exactly, a clue of some sort, when she sees it. A white square on the lawn. She picks it up and, even in the hazy light, sees enough to recognize. It's a small piece of paper, definitely torn out from a book, with only a few legible lines beneath smudges and a fat, still-wet drop of blood.

It is impossible to say how first the idea entered my brain; but once conceived, it haunted me day and night. Poe's name at the top of the page.

She takes a big breath and walks into the woods. It seems like a much longer walk than she'd done less than an hour ago. Everything has warped slightly, each tree and branch swaying in the breeze and every sound twisted and angry. The birdsongs are gone and it is much darker here than in her backyard. The trees are watching her and whispering about her, she can feel it.

She's breathing heavy, somewhere between scared and excited. Even *if* she finds this wounded stranger who stole her books, who was in her *room*, what is she going to say to him? What is she supposed to do?

She looks up and sees her dreamcatcher turning in the wind. She had been right near her and Kelly's old fort earlier but not even noticed. She sees now that a dead tree has been dragged on top to make a sort of shelter, obscuring it. Deep breath. Courage.

He doesn't see her at first. He is sitting on the mossy rock with his back to her. His leg is bent across his lap and he is rubbing something on it, hissing in pain. She can see only the back of his head, his brown-red shoulder-length hair knotted in loose dreads, the shadow of his outline large against the night. Even sitting down, she can tell he's tall, wide-shouldered, much bigger than her. He could easily overpower her but, somehow, she's not afraid of him. She doesn't know what to say at first.

"What do you want?" he asks without turning towards her. It is a voice that hasn't spoken in a very long time, gruff and crackling, quiet and low.

What *does* she want? What does she expect of him, this wounded book thief in the woods? She wants to help him, but she doesn't know how.

"You took my books."

She steps closer, cautiously. He turns and flinches, like he's afraid of her. Ridiculous; she should be the one afraid of a mysterious stranger in the woods. But she's not. Ari kneels by the roots of the fallen tree that obscures the small nook underneath where his things are stashed. Her things, actually. She can see her brown leather-bound volume of *Sherlock Holmes* in the place where the rock and tree meet. Her mom's pan, a dozen other books, all hers.

"Why'd you take those? What do you need them for?"

He won't look her in the eye. His wide shoulders are hunched, head down, face obscured by his thick unwashed hair. His clothes are so filthy that she can't tell what color they used to be. He is wearing a long-sleeved crew neck shirt spotted with holes, fabric worn thin around the collar and loose, dark pants held up by twine.

He whispers something that she thinks might have been *Sorry.*

His right leg is red and bloody, sticky with dark clots. His dirty workman's pants are torn from the upper thigh past the knee. His dark eyes are scared, like a wounded animal's, darting from her to his stash and back, skittish. It's clear he hasn't spoken to another human being in a long time. Must be lonely, she thinks. Like her.

"Are you…are you OK?" she asks, leaning in a little.

His response is terse: "Fine."

"You don't look fine. What happened to you?" She keeps her distance, still staying a few feet away, afraid to touch him. His gaze goes down to his leg, which is swollen and puffy.

Ari shines her flashlight on it. She can see yellow-purple fuzz at the edge of a deep wound, spanning from his thigh to just below his knee. The edge is crusted with dark bits of blood. An off-white film circles the edge of the jagged cut. She doesn't know much about First Aid, but even she can tell that wound is definitely infected.

"Attack," he murmurs.

"By what?"

He is quiet for long enough that she doesn't think he's going to answer. Then he says, "Coyote."

"A coyote did that?" She sits and scooches closer on the rock, slipping for a second on the damp moss, wiping dirt on her hands. He nods.

She looks up into his eyes, his pupils dilated. They're younger than she expects. He has a bushy copper-colored beard, but his eyes make him look softer than his outer gruffness. She can't place his age, even within decades.

"Did you kill it?" she asks softly. A part of her reminds herself that she doesn't know this strange man in the woods who entered her home without being invited. But a louder voice within her reminds her that he's alone, too, and hurt. And even if she is slow, she can still probably outrun someone with a leg like that, if she has to.

Again, he nods. He looks down at the leg, like he is ashamed.

"How?"

He points to the small cave dug out underneath the rock, blocked off by the rotten tree that was haphazardly placed a few feet away. She can see a sharp pointy stick on the rock there, by the small entrance. Even from a few feet away, she can see the sticky blood-red tip.

"Where is it? The coyote?" She isn't sure she really wants to know, but it is the first question that comes to her.

"Ate it."

She doesn't want to think about eating a coyote or how that would even work. She never even knew there were coyotes back here in the woods so close to her house. The woods where she used to come all the time. Something about that unsettles her.

"You live out here, don't you? Behind our house?"

He shrugs again, his broad shoulders a question mark.

"Why?"

He pauses, then says, "Got nowhere else to go."

"No family? Friends? Nobody?"

His eyes meet hers, hold her gaze. "Nope. Not anymore."

They're both silent for what feels like a long time before he says, "I just don't seem to fit in anywhere…out there. Here, things make more sense. Nature. Just…surviving. Out there never made much sense to me."

She nods, as if she understands. There's a lot that doesn't make sense to her either. If she was good at stuff like hunting and building fires and…skinning coyotes…maybe she'd choose a life like this too, with just books and the woods and your basic needs. No Kelly and Brendan or Mom or Joe or her dad or the stupid baby. *Just surviving.* She thinks she gets it.

"Do you need anything?" She asks. "Besides…" She gestures to the pile of books and few household items, the gauze, rubbing alcohol.

"I've got what I need."

"I could bring you books sometimes, if you want," she offers. "But I want that one back," she gestures to *Sherlock Holmes*. "It's special."

He nods and waves his hand toward the book.

"I'm supposed to write a book report about that one," she points at *The Giver*. "But you can read it first, if you want. Maybe we can talk about it. You could...help me with my report?"

He pauses, then nods, almost imperceptibly. "I was never great with that sorta thing," he says. "School. But I like to read."

"Me too." It's one of the only things she feels good at.

A few moments of silence that's not uncomfortable.

"You gonna tell?" he almost whispers.

"No," she shakes her head. "Promise." And she knows she won't.

She scooches toward him, just a few feet away, and they both look at the trees in front of them, the last of the light flickering through their branches. Her dreamcatcher spins on the branch, filtering everything bad out of her dreams.

No Strings Attached

Carmen hadn't been touched since she'd left Ricky for good. The bruises on her neck, ribcage, and hip had faded to a soft brown, like birthmarks, all she had left to show of him. She wanted to scrub him from her skin. She wanted to be wanted again. But the prospect of flirting with strangers at a bar or a party was far too terrifying to bear, and the dating apps were just a bunch of creepy trolls, so she turned to the *Seeking* section of the free paper, which she and her friends used to read aloud to each other for fun in high school. They dared each other to reply but never did.

She got off the bus in front of the apartment complex, which was a series of connected brick buildings that formed a U. She checked the address on her phone again and rang the doorbell of 301C. She had come wearing normal clothes, a gray crop top and baggy jeans, no jewelry or make-up. She didn't want to seem too desperate, but she also didn't want to be too drab, so she was wearing a black lace bra and a matching thong. It would have seemed weird to just wear some old granny panties or something. She wasn't sure how to dress for something like this.

She rang the doorbell again and considered walking away, going back home, going anywhere but these strangers' apartment, when the door opened and a petite white woman answered. Her features were small and delicate, like a doll's, her make-up elegant, her brown hair perfectly straight and glossy. She looked like someone used to getting what she wanted. She shook Carmen's hand and invited her in. The formality was a bit awkward, considering. A fit man with graying hair appeared from a doorway and introduced himself as Bill. "Thanks for coming," he said. "We've been looking forward to this." Carmen didn't know what to say. What was she doing here? Was it too late to leave?

Their apartment wasn't large and the clutter made it look smaller, organized clutter, things she imagined they bought on trips across the world, useless things. Masks covered with real fur, painted vases with dried flowers in them, candlesticks, wooden figurines, wooden bowls.

Bill offered her something to drink. She accepted a finger of bourbon, neat, to give her a little courage, something to do with her hands. He poured one for himself and drank it quickly.

"So, are you a student?" he asked.

"No," Carmen said, "not anymore." She didn't say she'd dropped out of college when Ricky made her. He'd said it wasn't worth the money, that she needed to pull her weight around here, but Carmen knew he'd been jealous of her having her own thing, especially one where she interacted with other guys. He was always grilling her after class about who she'd talked to. She knew he didn't like her having something that was just hers, a world apart from him. She couldn't go back now. Bill didn't press further.

The woman sat on the couch and watched her sip her drink. Carmen could feel her eyes on her.

"Do you have a boyfriend? Or girlfriend?" The woman asked. She didn't seem very interested in the answer.

"No," Carmen said. "Not anymore."

It was hard to remember a time when things had been good with Ricky. There were photos of them having fun, laughing, that taunted her from her Instagram page, but they seemed like they were of someone else. She couldn't remember being that person. One of them had been her profile picture—a shot of him hugging her from behind, both mid laugh, sharing some private joke she couldn't remember. Her new profile picture is of her cat.

When their glasses were empty, Bill led them both into the bedroom. His wife sat down on the edge of the neatly made bed. Carmen waited for one of them to make the first move. She wasn't sure how these things were supposed to go. She'd never done anything like this, answered a stranger's ad in the personal section. *Seeking fit and discreet woman, 18-25, for play with married couple*, the ad had said. *No strings attached.*

Bill locked the door behind him with a key. The click of the lock reminded Carmen of the prison doors shutting behind her when she used to visit her father, the clang and echo of heavy metal doors clicking shut, locking her in. Though this door wasn't nearly as heavy, the lock couldn't possibly have been as loud, yet it was, that small sound echoing in her ears, reverberating in her body. She felt just as trapped in that room as she did in the prison. It was why she'd stopped visiting at twelve, that feeling.

Bill moved towards Carmen with precision. Her body stiffened and she took a step back. The seriousness of the situation weighed heavy on her; she was locked in a room with strangers who could do anything to her. Hadn't that been the point? No strings attached? She'd thought a married couple would be safer somehow. It didn't seem so exciting anymore.

Bill closed the distance between them, gripped her hips firmly, pulled her towards him, and pushed her onto the bed beside his wife, who didn't move. "I want to watch you two," he said, serious and commanding. This didn't feel like the play that had been advertised.

The woman turned to Carmen and slowly lowered her legs to either side of her and squeezed her hips close, ran her hand up Carmen's stomach to her breast, pulled up her shirt, slid her hand under her lace bra. Carmen tingled at her cold touch. The small woman moved mechanically, exact and lifeless. She sucked at Carmen's nipple, ran her teeth over it. Carmen froze.

Bill didn't take his eyes off her and she returned his stare while his wife's lips brushed up Carmen's collarbone, neck, chin. Her kisses were light and impersonal, her lips barely pressing against Carmen's skin. "Bite her," Bill said, and she did, hard, on her shoulder. Carmen could feel the indentation of the woman's teeth on her skin. Like Ricky, she had left herself imprinted on Carmen's body.

The woman dug her manicured nails into Carmen's breasts, pulled her thick hair, bit her lip, hard. Carmen tried to protest but the woman kissed her hard, Bill placed his hands firmly on her hips and held her down, and she couldn't pull away. He unbuttoned and yanked her jeans down in one fluid motion, climbed on top of her, squeezed her hips between his, his hard cock pressing against her pubic bone through her underwear. He pushed himself against her, hard. He held her arms above her head, gripped her wrists tight and dug her bracelet into her skin. The woman's teeth sank into Carmen's breast, leaving teeth marks that bloomed on Carmen's skin. She tried to protest but Bill covered her mouth with one hand and still held both her wrists in the other.

The beating of her heart against her chest—a drum—pounded its rhythm in her, faster and faster, echoing in her bones. Ba-DUM-da-DUM-da-DUM. Too fast, too loud. Her voice stuck like a bone in her throat, choking her, like the time Ricky had held her throat too tight, the fingerprints still there, faint. Words wouldn't come.

It was like the first time with Ricky. He'd pinned her against the bathroom sink, gripped her hips and pulled her forward, thrust himself into her, pounded her tailbone against the metal sink, leaving a bruise that made it hurt to sit. She knew how to hurt. She knew how to give in.

She gripped the edges of the mattress as hard as she could, dug in, held in the pain. She remembered the feeling of the knife sinking into Ricky's flesh, the soft way his stomach had given in to it, the rush of blood as she pulled it out. How she had left him there to bleed out. No strings attached.

How We Feed Ourselves

First, we feed from our mother—blood, then milk. We feed at her breast and then, at her table. She sustains us. Most mothers feed their children all their lives. These mothers offer their love, food they made with their hands. I didn't have a mother like that. I had a mother whose appetite for self-destruction swallowed us all whole.

"Is she ever coming back?" my seven-year-old brother Cal asked me after she'd been gone for three days, no warning, leaving me, at twelve, to feed us both. She didn't leave a note or money for food or anything.

We were squeezed into Cal's twin bed in the Section 8 apartment we'd been renting for a few months. It wasn't much but it had walls and our own space, two bedrooms so Cal and I shared a room. There was nothing on the walls, but you could see cracks crawling up the wall like vines, bluish-black mold at the edges of the windows.

I wanted to tell him she'd be back any day now, that everything would be alright. Instead, I said, "I don't know, Cal. I don't know," and he fell asleep in my arms.

All week, I made sure to grab extra apples and oranges and cookies from the free school breakfasts and lunches, which made up our dinners. By the weekend we'd eaten up our stash, so I stole a bag of Utz's potato chips (it turned out to be pickle flavor) and two Snickers bars from the bodega down the street. I ducked out before Mr. Diaz behind the counter could see me. I felt bad because he was nice but what else was I supposed to do? The chips and Snickers lasted us two more days, until our mother finally came back after dark, bearing turkey and American cheese slices. She offered no explanation or apology. We pretended like nothing was wrong.

Our mother's unemployment checks mostly bought pills, Wild Turkey, and Beefaroni we had to make last for days. When she wasn't working, Cal and I survived on Slim Jims and the pickled eggs from a jar by the bodega register, four for a dollar. We squatted in apartment buildings with no heat or power and ate cold black beans on stale tortillas. When there was a stovetop or hotplate, my mother made "stone soup," which meant whatever she could find—beans, onion skins, the ends of carrots, leftover hamburger. I learned to cook early, simple things, when we got a few dollars: scrambled eggs, pasta, chili. I fed us all.

I wanted to be the kind of mother who could feed her child, to offer my love in loaves of bread I baked myself, in the carrots I dug from soil, in warm things pulled from the oven. I wanted to work for my daughter's love, to earn it. I boiled and mashed sweet potatoes and frozen peas once she graduated from my milk. I rolled out dough for pies and baked cookies to celebrate report cards. I mixed pancake batter on Sunday mornings and watched the ladlesful expand on the griddle. I learned to dice, mince, and sauté, to slice and boil and roast. I taught myself these things. I wish I had family recipes that had been passed down, instructions for how to feed my child. I would give my daughter that.

Now, at fourteen, my daughter, Maya, is disappearing. She stopped eating gradually. It started with her not taking seconds like she usually did, then declining dessert, then cutting out snacks altogether. When we went to the grocery store, she stopped asking for mint Milanos (her favorite) or Cheez-Its, or any of the things to which I knew I should say no but usually caved. She stopped eating the Parker House rolls I often served with dinner, which she used to take two of. Then she stopped eating the sides, mashed potatoes or rice or pasta. She cut her meat meticulously, just a few small bites. She took her time chewing. Often, she just sat at the table staring at her food or watching us eat. Her anger seemed to turn inwards. She was quick to criticize herself, constantly examining herself in any reflective surface and finding herself wanting. She became quiet, unlike the Maya I had known.

After about a week of watching our teenage daughter refusing to eat, I brought it up with Michael one night before bed.

"She's just going through a phase," he said. "She'll get over it." His tone said 'drop it' so I did.

Already, she was pale, sluggish, irritable. She withdrew and responded curtly when asked a question, giving no more than one or two-word answers. My vibrant daughter was fading, a shadow of herself.

When I was growing up, Mom would take us with her to the park to panhandle. She probably thought she'd have a better chance with kids by her side. The trick was to look them in the eyes. Most people couldn't say no to a hungry child.

She'd occasionally get work at a fast-food joint or a retail store but would inevitably lose it when she was too fucked up to make it in. Shopping on pay days was my favorite because we each got to pick out candy. I always chose peanut M&Ms and ate them slowly, one at a time, to make them last. Cal preferred Twix and always scarfed them down right away. We'd eat our treats while Mom and her friends partied in whatever apartment we were living in at the time. No one cared if we stayed up late. Then there were the in-between periods when we relied on the food shelf and WIC, when we'd have dinners of Wonder Bread and peanut butter all week, when we slept on her friends' floors. Those were the times she'd sulk around, and everything got her down. We knew not to ask for anything then, that the answer would surely be *no*.

Mom, Cal, and I continued to bounce around Brooklyn and I had to change schools several times. I rarely got my homework done and fell behind. The principal told me I'd have to repeat ninth grade. That was around the time I met Jared at a bar that would serve anybody. I didn't have any money the night we met, but I only had to stand at the bar for a minute before he came up and bought me a Heineken, which seemed fancy to me then. He was in his twenties, a DJ, which made him sound cool. He fucked me propped up on the dirty bathroom sink. It felt good to be wanted.

We began meeting in the park during my lunch period to smoke joints and fool around in the public bathroom, then I started skipping class to see him. I was going to fail freshman year for the second time, but Jared convinced me I didn't need school and that we should leave the city instead.

He got a job at the racetrack in Yonkers, only a twenty-five-minute Metro North train ride from Grand Central, he said. I'd been living in Mom's boyfriend's one-bedroom apartment, so I jumped at the chance to have a place of our own. I wanted to bring Cal with us, but Jared wouldn't go for it. We couldn't afford to take care of a kid, he said. He told me we could come get him once I got a job, and we'd saved up a little money. In the meantime, he promised Cal could visit, if he could somehow come up with the subway fare and $13 train ticket each way. But he didn't come. By the time I went back to look for him, a few months later, he and my mother were gone. She'd broken up with her boyfriend and he didn't know how to find her.

Jared took to spending his spare time at the track, too, and lost most of the money I made working at an all-night diner under the table. He would come home drunk and empty-handed and find some mistake I'd supposedly made, like not cleaning the dishes well enough or forgetting to turn the heat down when I left the apartment and flip out at me. Once he even threw a glass at me, which shattered against the wall. Though he often complimented my looks and made me feel pretty, he also told me no one else would want me, that I wasn't smart enough to support myself without him. I wanted to leave him but didn't have anywhere to stay, anyone else to take care of me. I believed he was right. I woke up crying more than once.

I started saving up money, hiding it in my underwear drawer. Eventually I told him he had to quit gambling or I'd leave. He didn't quit. One of the other waitresses at the diner offered to rent me her spare room on the cheap. One night, after he'd been drinking and lost big at the track, he pushed me, I tripped over the coffee table and landed on my wrist, snapping it. I locked myself in our room and called the waitress, who came and picked me up in her Civic. She beeped the horn from in front of our building and I walked out with everything I could fit in my backpack, holding my swollen wrist, and never went back. This was before cell phones and he didn't know where to reach me. I don't know if he tried.

Worried that Jared would find me at the diner, I quit and my friend drove me all around town to look for other restaurant work. I borrowed her tight black dress and heels, hoping they'd make me look older than sixteen. I was turned down at six places before the manager of a cafe looked me up and down, leering, and offered me a job on the spot. That's how I met Michael, the twenty-eight-year-old insurance agent who came in for the soup of the day and a black coffee most afternoons. He always sat in my section and gave me a big tip. It was months before he finally asked me out by writing his number on the receipt. I couldn't believe a guy like that, a guy with a grown-up job and a college degree, would want me.

I moved in with him after just a few months. He rented a condo in the fancier town of Bronxville, just one stop past Yonkers on Metro North, but seemingly worlds away. Instead of the racetrack and liquor stores, Bronxville had sushi restaurants and stores that called themselves "boutiques," which meant expensive. We went out to eat most weekends. We were comfortable.

I couldn't believe the way my life had changed so drastically in just a few short months. It was like I'd stepped out of my skin as if it were a pair of jeans and become someone new. Michael had saved me. Only a year after we started dating, one night we were eating at the café on my break, and he got down on one knee right there in front of everybody and proposed. Of course, I said yes. I wanted a different life than the one I'd known.

It wasn't long before we had Maya. We traded the condo in for a bigger house with a yard. We got a dog. I didn't talk about my old life, never told my husband about living with no heat or water, staying in one place for no more than a few months. I thought by burying the past, I could erase it.

Maya was insatiable. When she was a baby, she fed constantly, so that my nipples were cracked and raw. It was a relief when she started eating solid foods, avocados and applesauce, then, fistfuls of Goldfish and animal crackers that she tucked away in her cheeks like a chipmunk. She constantly demanded snacks until she got old enough to make them herself. She was a very active child, and, as she got older, competed in tennis and field hockey, ran in her spare time. I had to keep the house stocked with crackers and her favorite sharp cheddar, tortilla chips and salsa, honey-wheat pretzels, carrot sticks and hummus, trail mix, bananas, peanut butter, Greek yogurt. She usually went to the store with me to make sure I got it all right. She liked to compare brands, read nutrition labels, take her time deciding which apple looked ripest. She often helped me in the kitchen, unevenly dicing garlic or onions. I wanted to teach her to feed herself.

She was full of vitality but was a difficult child from the time she was a toddler, prone to mood swings and a violent temper. One teacher told me she had anger problems after she smashed another kid's block tower when he wouldn't let her help. She was like that, an only child, used to getting her way. A live wire, Michael's mother called her.

I think Maya's eating issues must be my fault, at least in part. I think of all the times I complained about being too fat, worthless, ugly in front of her, despite my average size. How must that have made her feel about her own body? I taught my daughter to hate herself and I would have to live with that. I had thought I could be so much better.

I want to spoon my love into her mouth. I want her to swallow it, to let me feed her, as my body once fed her. I want her to hold the warm coals of my love in the empty cave of her belly, to keep her fire burning.

One dinner, Maya nibbled slowly on an undressed piece of lettuce, making it last. She didn't engage in our conversation or even look up from her lettuce. She was fixated on it. Eventually, Michael lost patience.

"You'll sit there as long as you have to until every bite on your plate is gone," he said sternly through clenched teeth. He didn't raise his voice but somehow, that was even worse, like he'd passed anger and moved on to something else. She said nothing and looked down at her lap. She didn't move.

"Is the meal your mother made not good enough for you?" Michael pressed her. "Don't you appreciate this food we've provided? We work our butts off for you, young lady." I felt like I was being chastised, too. Through tears she said, softly, "I'm sorry." She wouldn't look him in the eyes.

Michael eventually gave up and went to watch TV, which I could hear blaring from the living room. I sat with her in silence, in the dark, until ten o'clock, when she got up and went to bed without saying anything.

Maya has had an independent streak since she was a baby. She'd always push Michael and me away, try to do things for herself. Once, when she was four, we had both tried desperately to pull a splinter from her foot before she had finally got fed up, grabbed the tweezers from me, and pulled the thing out herself. She always wanted to solve everything on her own. When she was a toddler, she insisted on dressing herself, buttoning the wrong buttons and refusing to let me help her fix them. At six, when she fell out of a tree she was climbing and broke her arm, she pretended to be fine for an entire afternoon before admitting how much it hurt. She doesn't ask for help, even when she needs it.

I know she puts a lot of pressure on herself to be perfect, and, I have to admit, maybe I put a little too much pressure on her, too. The thing is, I know what it's like to live in squalor, supported only by a mostly unemployed mother without a high school diploma. My daughter won't live like that. She will graduate, go to college, succeed, be more than a waitress like me. My concerns for her have been focused so much on the future, what she will be and do, that I failed to really see the person changing in front of me.

She's lost so much weight that her clothes are shapeless and baggy on her already-thin frame. Her bones have become sharper, more pronounced. Her face looks hollow. She's slowed down. She's cold all the time and has started wearing two or three sweaters, layer upon layer, to warm herself. Her skin has developed a film of dark, downy hair. I've tried talking to her about it, but she dismisses me every time with "I'm fine." She isn't fine. None of us is fine.

I took her to the doctor, who said she was dangerously underweight and suggested I buy a scale to track her weight week-to-week. You'd think I was torturing Maya, making her get on it. I hated it as much as she did, I'm sure. I had to hold my arms tightly around her gangly body and shuffle her onto the scale. She begged—*nononononon-onono*—but I insisted. Finally, she gave in once the numbers started to tick down, curious. She'd lost twenty-seven pounds from her last physical, just a few months before. Field hockey kept her slim and she didn't have twenty-seven pounds to spare. This was proof there was a problem, as if I couldn't see it in her bones. Maya's pediatrician referred us to a nutritionist and an adolescent psychologist.

On Wednesdays I had to pick Maya up from school early and drive her the forty-five minutes into the city for her appointments, which meant taking Wednesday afternoons off from the restaurant and not getting paid. This made things even more tense between Michael and me. He didn't trust psychotherapy and thought it was a waste of time and money. He thought it was as simple as just making her eat again. He was worried about paying for college, while I was worried about keeping her alive. It felt like she was slipping away, sinking into a dark place.

She was so fragile, so quick to be wounded. She cried most days over the smallest things, exploding a bottle of seltzer in the kitchen, getting a B on a test, and of course, our trying to force her to eat. Michael lost his patience with her, yelled a lot, blamed her for putting us through this, which made her fall deeper into herself.

I walked into the kitchen to hear his anger filling up the room, her cowering in the corner.

"Don't you see what you're doing to your mother? Do you know how selfish you are?" he shouted.

Maya was crying, that way she has of crying silently, red-faced and heaving. It makes her look younger, reminds me of days when her problems were easier to solve.

I know the therapy and nutritionist appointments have been stressful for my daughter, the anxiety that comes with her weekly weigh-ins, having to face the parts of herself she's trying to bury. I understand that, having a dark shame to hide—my mother, my past, leaving my eleven-year-old brother behind, losing touch. I want to be better for my daughter.

I wanted to do something to cheer Maya up, to offer some relief from the loaded silence that sits between us on the drive home from the city. I had never thought about how many things revolve around food, how I had always, without thinking about it, celebrated my daughter's accomplishments or comforted her disappointments with sugary treats, that I didn't really know how to celebrate her without food. A trip to the bakery that makes those cinnamon rolls she loves would not comfort Maya after the indignity she faces every week, laying bare the darkest parts of herself, the parts that hurt. She wouldn't, or couldn't, tell me what was wrong, what was hurting. I couldn't help her.

Maya would shiver in the thin gown that revealed her bones, standing on the scale, waiting for judgment to be passed. Was it a gaining week or a losing week? Either way was bad. She'd be reprimanded by the doctor for losing more weight, not keeping to the rigid nutritional plan the doctor had given us. If she'd lost weight, Michael would punish her, not letting her hang out with her friends, though she'd lately withdrawn from them, anyway. Or, if she had gained and gotten the doctor's approval, she would be ashamed, furious, even, turning her hatred inwards. I wanted to tell her it would get better, to wrap my arms around her emaciated body, but she would pull away from me every time.

We had an hour to kill between appointments, so we started going to a coffee shop in mid-town in between them. The coffee shop was trendy, one wall brick and covered with chalk drawings. It was always full of young people, artsy types, college students. I held on to some small hope at first that Maya would order a large hot chocolate with whipped cream or ask for a scone, but all she'd have was plain black tea, no honey or sugar or milk.

I saw the woman the first time we went there, sitting on the steps next to the coffee shop entrance, her body hidden beneath blankets, a cardboard sign on her lap with *Anything Helps* written in Sharpie, coffee cup with a handful of change at her feet. I probably wouldn't have noticed her if Maya hadn't asked for a dollar to give. She's big-hearted, always trying to help other people. The woman looked up to thank her and I saw familiar eyes.

I only saw her face for a few seconds that first time, but those eyes—Maya's eyes, blue and bright and hungry—gave her away. She'd aged badly, skin pockmarked and red, wrinkles weighing heavily around her eyes, wisps of gray hair sticking out from under her too-big knit hat. It was hard to tell under all the blankets, but she looked like she'd gained a lot of weight. I could see it in her bloated face. If she recognized me, she didn't show it. Unable to move, I stood there and stared until Maya called "*Mo-om*" and I followed her into the coffee shop.

My daughter has never met my mother. Neither has my husband, for that matter. I had no family at our wedding. The only family I have is the one we made. I haven't talked to my mother since I left. I wouldn't know how to find her, even if I'd wanted to.

What did I have to say to her? I was a different person than the one she had known. I left home when I was barely more than Maya's age because I wasn't strong enough to watch my mother kill herself. Now, my daughter won't feed herself or let me feed her. I have to watch her kill herself, and I'm still not strong enough.

Maya and I sat in silence for most of the hour, sipping our drinks on the coffee shop couch, and people-watching. I could see her taking mental notes, about what, I'm not sure. She's an observant kid. I'd found us a seat near the window, hoping I could catch a glimpse of the woman who I was almost positive was my mother, but I could just see the part of her blankets where her feet would be, stretched out on the sidewalk. When we left, I slowed down and tried to look at her carefully, but she just stared at the sidewalk. I put another dollar in her cup.

Each Wednesday, I made sure I had a few dollar bills on me. As we approached her, Maya would look up at me, asking without saying anything, and I would silently hand her a few bills. I didn't tell her who I thought the woman was. My mother was my secret, my own private shame. I was used to being embarrassed by her, had been for much of my adolescence, by her unkemptness, her outbursts.

After a couple of weeks, I started writing on dollar bills and sticking them in my wallet to give her. My initials, my phone number, my birthday. I wanted to say *It was your fault*, or *You drove me away*, or *You were the real reason Cal had to suffer.* It was her fault I'd had to leave him behind, her fault that we'd lost touch until I found him on Facebook a few years ago, all her fault.

I'd searched his name and come up with a dozen profiles, some featuring dogs or vague silhouettes, but I recognized him almost instantly, his far-off expression, those familiar eyes. I sent him a message, inviting him to our house. It turned out he still lived in Brooklyn, about an hour and a half on the train. Maya was eleven then, the age he'd been when I'd last seen him. I could still see that child in him, that scared, lonely child. I wanted to cry for that child, to hold him close. When we hugged, it was like hugging a stranger. We'd spent more time apart than we had together.

"So, Cal," Michael had said over pork chops, "What are you up to these days?" As if they were old friends who'd fallen out of touch. Cal shrugged and mumbled, "This and that." He didn't say much the whole dinner. He didn't ask questions about our lives.

He was twitchy, constantly moving, and unnaturally thin. I could see his bones, just like with Maya now, his gaunt cheeks, hungry eyes. He looked like so many of my mom's boyfriends, skinny addicts, wiry men who couldn't be relied upon—there one day, gone the next. He looked like what I remember of my father before he left, slender and barely there.

Cal cut his meat violently, scraping his knife on the ceramic plate.

"Where are you living?" I asked, imagining the dumps we'd lived in as kids, hoping his life wasn't a repeat of our childhood.

"Bed-Stuy," he said. I wanted for him to elaborate and when he didn't, I asked, "On your own?"

He shook his head.

"I got a girlfriend," he said, "She's got a kid. He's nine."

So he was a father figure? We hadn't had one growing up, not for any period of time, anyway. I wanted to ask about the kid, the girlfriend, what kind of life they had, but he didn't offer details.

We were eating the coffee cake I'd made for dessert by the time I finally got up the courage to ask what I'd most wanted to.

"Do you know where Mom is these days?"

At first, I thought he hadn't heard me. He was focused intently on his cake, picking up every crumb.

"Nope. Last time I saw her a DCF worker was taking me away and she was freaking out. She was yelling and throwing shit and making a whole scene. I don't know if she ever tried to get me back after that. She just kind of disappeared."

"Don't you want to know, though?"

I didn't mention that I'd searched for her, too, but there was no digital trace of her. I'd even Googled obituaries, but the only person I found with her name was twenty years older than her and had a family she'd left behind. Then again, who would have written her obituary? Who would have paid for it?

"Not really," he said. "I got nothing to say to her."

Though I resented her for the childhood we had, too, I also ached for her in a way that shocked me, especially since I had become a mother. I couldn't imagine Maya never wanting to see me again. Plus, I felt a desperate need to know. It was a need that I thought he might share.

Cal looked embarrassed when he asked me for money as I drove him to the train station. I wrote him a check. I felt I owed him that. Then he disappeared, didn't respond to my texts or Facebook messages. He was gone from my life again, the last bridge to the life we'd had, once.

Now, when I see her by the coffee shop, I have an urge to touch this woman, my mother, to let her hug me like she did when I was small. That's one thing I remember: she was a good hugger. Maya won't let me hug her anymore. She pulls away if I try to put an arm around her, flinches if I put my hand on her back.

One Wednesday morning before I picked Maya up from school for her appointments, I cooked. I diced onions, minced garlic, chopped bell peppers, carefully diced hot chiles. I let three-bean chili simmer in the crockpot while I baked corn bread from scratch, mixing in canned corn. I'm no gourmet chef, but Michael loves my chili. I made chocolate chip cookies, which reminded me of how Maya had loved to eat cookie dough when she was younger; there would hardly be any left to bake. I slathered the bread with butter and scooped the chili into a thermos, grabbed a spoon, and packed it all up. I didn't know what to say to my mother; nothing seemed like enough, but I could feed her, at least.

This time, there was no one on the steps, no sign, no paper coffee cup. I'd missed my chance and let my family get away again. In the coffee shop, cupping a hot mug in her hands, Maya said softly, "You didn't do anything wrong, Mom. I want you to know that. It's not your fault. You didn't do anything bad or anything."

I didn't know what to say to that. She's wrong, I thought; of course it was my fault. I hadn't been good enough at loving her, at holding her close. I left my own mother, who couldn't take care of herself and who's who-knows-where now, and I can't feed my own daughter. I reached for her bony hand and she didn't pull away.

"It's nobody's fault, sweetie," I said in my best motherly voice. "You're getting better. You're going to be OK. It's going to be OK."

"No," she said, looking down at our intertwined hands. "It's me. There's something wrong with me. I don't know what it is exactly. I'm just—broken. And I'm trying to be better, I want to be, I just—I can't. I can't do it, Mom."

She started to cry; ugly, heaving sobs.

"There's tissues in my purse," I pointed to the leather purse on the chair next to her. She reached in to grab a tissue and pulled out the Tupperware container of cookies. She wiped her eyes, took a cookie, and chewed it slowly, her eyes closed, taking her time with each bite.

Promise Me

My mother sent me the obituary from my hometown newspaper. She wanted to know if I'd talked to him since high school. I lied and said no. She asked if I knew what had happened. The obit didn't say. She wanted an explanation, but as is so often the case with these things, there wasn't one, at least not a satisfying one. I didn't tell her why I was coming home.

The service was in the Catholic church his mother attended, which he would have hated. When he was five or six PBRs deep, he would rant about the church's "hypocritical bullshit," how fools like his mother were taken for a ride. "I believe in the god of booze," he once professed, offering a bottle of cheap whiskey as a toast, "a forgiving god." His lack of faith and, more importantly, refusal to attend church with her was more disturbing to his mother than anything else. She and her late husband emigrated from Spain under Franco and their family had been devout Catholics for generations. I was surprised that the church even allowed her to have his funeral there. Maybe his mother really believed it was an accident.

I didn't want to go to the funeral. I hadn't spoken to him in almost a year and I knew no one would be happy to see me there. But I felt I owed it to him, so I packed the conservative black dress I'd worn to my father's funeral a decade earlier and boarded the plane back home. I feared his sister the most. She was the one who'd sent me a barrage of angry Facebook messages after I left. We were friends growing up, in Girl Scouts together. We used to play fairies in the woods behind my house.

She said it was my fault, that I'd broken his heart. She said I was heartless, that I only thought about myself. I didn't tell her how untrue that was. I drafted several replies before deleting them. I wanted to tell her he was broken before he'd come back into my life, that he'd already tried it once, though it didn't feel like my place to be the one to tell her. I wanted to tell her how I'd been broken, too, that I was barely hanging on and badly needed someone to take care of me. I wanted to tell her how his love had smothered me, was too much, how I wanted to be alone again, far away in my own city. In the end, I couldn't shatter her perception of her big brother, so I quietly accepted the blame. I chose not to block her so I could feel her ire and bury it deep.

In kindergarten, he tried to kiss my cheek in Circle every morning. It was a game. We had to sit on small squares of duct tape stuck to the carpet, evenly spaced, and I would have my friends sit on the squares on either side of me to protect me, but he'd usually find his way to me anyway. When he'd kiss my cheek, I'd pretend it disgusted me, but I liked the warmth. It would be years before I'd be kissed by anyone again.

I'd been fired from my job teaching poetry at a small college. My poetry classes had never been very popular and only three students signed up last term. Apparently, they all wrote unfavorable things on their teacher evaluations. The president told me they were "reprioritizing the department." After I got fired, I needed quiet and solitude to write in, so I returned to the sleepy mid-western town where I'd come from and lived in my old bedroom for a few months. In high school, I couldn't wait to get out of town, see the world, and I never expected myself to come back like this, thirty-seven and single, jobless, living at home. I reverted to my childhood self. I let my mother cook and do my laundry.

I first ran into him at the grocery store where he worked, then the library, then the pharmacy. I started to think maybe he was following me, and maybe he was, but it felt like hope, having someone excited to see me. One time I ran into him in the bookstore—he was looking for something by Pablo Neruda, he said. I didn't tell him Neruda had been a rapist, even wrote about it in his memoir. It seemed cruel to dispel his notions of his personal hero. We found a bilingual copy of Neruda's *The Captain's Verses* and I bought it for him. The next time I ran into him, he asked me for coffee and told me he'd read the book, cover to cover. He said he found it a bit sappy, but the rhythm in Spanish was pretty good. I admitted I didn't speak or read Spanish, so I only knew the translations, though, I made sure to note, I could infer some words based on their proximity to French, both being Romance languages and all. "You have to read him in Spanish," he insisted. I agreed to dinner at his place, where he would read me Neruda in Spanish.

We would see each other a handful more times before I felt stifled by him, by my mother, by being home. I didn't see a future there. I didn't see a future with him.

One time, he was trying to get my attention and I was engrossed in *The Captain's Verses,* which he was using to teach me Spanish. Poetry Spanish, as he said. He kept repeating my name and I kept saying, "In a minute," until, finally, he ripped the book from my hands and flung it across his small bedroom, tearing the Spanish side of "Tu Risa" ("Your Laughter").

I wore my hair down, the way he liked it best. He liked running his fingers through it, twisting a curl between his thumb and pointer finger. I wore the necklace he'd given me for our one-month anniversary (which he thought was worth celebrating, convinced as he was that me returning home was his happily ever after), almost-certainly-not-real gold with a ruby pendant, my birthstone and a color I generally loathed. Once again, I didn't have the heart to tell him. I could tell it was a big deal to him. Even if the gold wasn't real, it probably cost more than he made in a month. He was prone to doing things like that, making irresponsible purchases, especially when it came to me. He wanted to be able to shower me with extravagant things he imagined I wanted, take me out to fancy dinners, "treat me like a princess," he said. I never wanted to be a princess, his or anyone's.

Funerals make me uncomfortable: the formality, the awkwardness of strangers pretending they were closer to the dead person than they really were. My father's funeral was filled with old coworkers and Army buddies I'd never met, who hadn't seen or spoken to him in years. I was supposed to be grateful to them for coming, supposed to thank them and hug them, comfort *them*, as my mother did. But I wanted to scream at them, *You didn't even know him! Where were you when he died alone in the hospital, when his heart finally gave out? Where were you?* And now I am one of those people the family doesn't want to see, who they will look at with disdain, disgust, wonder why I am there. I am going for him, I told myself, not them. He asked me to promise that I would. I felt I owed it to him. The fact that I didn't see the message until it was too late is irrelevant.

I'd programmed G-mail to send his messages straight to the trash box, the dozens that came every few days, begging me to return. I'd had enough of them. Later, I'd wonder if my ghosting him contributed to the depths he couldn't crawl out of. When my mother sent me his obit, I searched my trash box and found a bunch of emails, including one from the day he died. The last one, sent the night he took the pills, asked me to promise I'd be at his funeral. "No one else really knows me," he wrote. "Promise me you'll be there to tell them who I was." He then signed off with the Neruda poem, in both English and Spanish (his own partial translation, having torn the Spanish side). As far as I'm aware, that email was the closest thing to a note that he left. I kept it up on my phone during the funeral. I couldn't stop reading it. It reminded me why I was there.

After a party in high school where he'd drunk too much and I was giving him a ride home, he sat in the front seat of my car, refusing to get out until I kissed him. He tried to climb over the center console, but I leaned away. *Please*, he begged, and I didn't relent. I finally honked the horn 'til he got out.

Nearly twenty years later, when I told him it was time for me to go back to my life, he deflated in that same way I remembered. *Why?* He asked. *Why?* He thought it had to be because of him, and it was a little bit, but it was more about me. I didn't fit into my life back home anymore. He told me he had nothing else to live for and I thought he was being dramatic.

I'd tried to slip into the pew in the back quietly, hoping not to be noticed. But I saw his sister's eyes on me from the front, saw her whisper to her mother, felt their stares. The service wasn't about him. It was given by a priest who didn't know him. He talked a lot about Jesus's charity towards others, which had nothing to do with him. There weren't many people there. When they invited anyone who wanted to say a few words to come to the podium and no one volunteered, I found my legs taking me there, all eyes on me, not sure of what I would say. "Promise me you'll tell them who I was," he had written. "Promise me I won't be forgotten."

I got to the podium, put on my glasses, and began to read the poem from his final email. "Take bread away from me, if you wish," I read, my voice sounding far away, like it must be coming from someone else. "Take air away, but do not take from me your laughter." I felt glares on me and tried to ignore them. They didn't really know him, flaws and all, only remembered what they wanted to, the revised history of someone who suffered. Though I couldn't save him, I could remember, at least.

The Bra Tree

With the chairlift stopped, the only sounds were the crack of branches snapping with the heft of the snow and the *swoosh* of sharp edges of skis and snowboards carving into the groomer's corduroy pattern below. If it weren't for the cold, Kristen wouldn't mind sitting for a few minutes. Her energy had been low since the surgery. She had noticed her limitations with more concern since her diagnosis, surveying every mood and feeling in her body as potential symptoms of a greater threat.

Their legs dangled over the trail, the weight of their skis and boots pulling their feet toward the snow thirty feet below. The chairlifts swayed, out of sync. The lift fit four, but it was just the two of them, spread out on the far sides of the chair so that a gap sat between them.

Kristen had an impulse to swing the chair to see if she could touch the lift tower—it looked so close—but she knew James would not be amused. He was already acting impatient, swinging his legs back and forth. When their kids were small enough to slip under the bar, she and James would each hold one of them back with their poles. Kristen was afraid of them plummeting.

This would be her first run all season. They'd both bought seasons passes, like every year, perhaps optimistically, but she hasn't felt up to it. She had expected things to go differently. She hadn't missed a season since her father taught her on the bunny hill when she was two, and she'd be damned if she was missing one now. James had been skeptical of her strength, but she'd insisted. More than anything, she wanted one more good day on the hill.

They used to compete for first tracks or skin up parts of the mountain the lift couldn't reach, but post-mastectomy, just putting on her gear tired her out. James insists her body is still her body, that he still loves all of it, but she knows something has changed between them. He reached for her in bed last night, ran his hands up her ribcage, but when they got to her missing breasts, she pulled away.

She was only forty-nine when her body declared war on her, her breasts casualties. Her body didn't belong to her anymore. It had become a foreign entity, enemy territory. She felt as though she were in a constant struggle against it.

As the coffee percolated this morning, he'd asked her yet again if she was *sure* she was up to skiing. She hadn't had much exercise these past few months, hadn't had the energy or the drive. But she wanted to ski the trail they met on, not sure of the condition she'd be in by next season. It's a double black diamond, way too steep and challenging for her right now, James said. He joked, "You could end up like I did the day we met," which meant with a broken leg from sliding on ice into a tree. She was on ski patrol then and rolled him onto the orange sled and skied him down. She had rescued him, but could he do the same for her?

The lift stopped by the bra tree, at the crest of the knoll before the lift's final ascent. An aspen, decorated with at least thirty bras, some new, shiny red satin or still-white lace, others shit-speckled and worn, nearly transparent with weather and age. She could see the colors dotted through the tree's otherwise-bare branches, a bright blur without her glasses.

In a forest of bare trees on either side of the lift line, the lace and satin stood out, flapping in the branches. Bras waved in the breeze like flags, taunting her. The bra tree was a bold symbol of femininity that existed at every mountain she'd skied since the late '70s or early '80s, when the trend spread and stuck. At mountains all over, bras waved through tree branches, proudly announcing, *We were here.*

The abandoned bras belonged to generations of women bold enough to shimmy out of them on the lift, toss them onto the tree, and ski down bare-breasted under their jackets. A bizarre rite of passage of the young and privileged that she never understood. She supposed they could have pocketed the old bras to toss onto the tree, but that seemed less exciting.

Her daughter once casually mentioned she'd tossed a bra up there as a teenager, which she immediately followed with, "*What?* Everybody does it." Kristen had felt a pang of envy then, a desire to be as brave as her daughter, a woman who could fling lingerie onto trees with abandon. She had never been a woman like that, even before.

"I swear, if they don't replace this old hunk of junk lift soon…" James' threat faded to a mumble.

That was a habit he had developed recently. He mumbled half a sentence and let it taper off unfinished. It irked her every time.

"It'll start up as soon as you stop complaining about it," she said.

The lift had only been stopped for about a minute, but time seemed to drag by with her legs dangling heavy in the air and the wind biting at her cheeks. She pulled her fleece neck warmer up and tucked it under her goggles to protect her face. The fleece quickly became matted with her spit; wet tufts of pink fluff stuck to her lips and tongue.

The cogs at the top of the tower ground slowly into gear and the lift sputtered back into action. She moved quickly. She tucked her gloves between her knees while she pulled her arms inside her jacket, sweater, and long-sleeved under shirt, like a turtle withdrawing into its shell. James said something, but she couldn't hear, shrugged into her jacket and sweater as she was. He might have asked what she was doing, as if it weren't clear.

They were almost past the tree. Her elbow got stuck for a second or two and she nearly missed her chance, but, just in time, she pulled her white cotton post-mastectomy bra out of her sleeve and tossed it into the branches with the others—inserts falling to the trail below—a white flag waving, perhaps surrendering, but to what?

Hands

The first time she was touched was in the dark. At a school assembly, the lights in the auditorium off so that they could see the video about drunk driving play on the projector screen above the stage. A hand was on her thigh and then between her legs. She tensed but didn't dare look at the boy the hand belonged to. She concentrated on the girl crying in the video, mascara running down her face, saying she wished she could take it back. Make it better again.

She'd only spoken to the boy in class. They had English and Bio together. Now, his hand crept up her thigh so slowly it was barely moving. She didn't flinch. His fingers followed the inside seam of her jeans. His knuckles pressed hard.

There, in squeaky seats, she chewed her lip until it stung, the hurt of it. She wanted him to press harder, harder. They didn't look at each other. A mother cried on screen, asked *why, why, why*. Mascara ran down the woman's puffy face. His thumb dug in and she sucked in air. She could hear the whole school breathing, in and out. Something unfamiliar stirred in her. Someone whispered and a teacher shushed them.

Acknowledgments

I owe a great deal of gratitude to so many folks for supporting me and making this book a reality. First, to the team at Rootstock—Sam and Jennifer—thank you so much for believing in this book and for all the work you do for the literary community in Vermont and beyond. To my cohort, classmates, and professors at the Bennington Writing Seminars—especially Claire Vaye Watkins, Manuel Gonzales, Jill McCorkle, and Alice Mattison, who helped shape these stories—thank you for making me a better writer. Special thanks to Eddy Ozoma for his multiple close reads, enthusiastic and invaluable feedback, and so many late nights talking books over Vermont beers. I also want to recognize Rebecca Rubenstein, Nicole Nelson, Beth Weinstock, Jen Wilson, Danielle Lawrence, Asia Calcagno, Jesse Woodward, Cristina Spencer, Jamie Moorefield, Matt Sosnow, Ellen vanNoppen, Kat Montgomery, and Jane Elkin for their friendship, astute feedback, and ongoing support.

To my Renegade Writers—how would I have gotten through the past decade-plus without you all? Shelagh Shapiro, Kim MacQueen, Patrick Dodge, Niels Rinehart, Lee Ann Cox, Angela Palm Hopkins, Jessica Hendry Nelson, Rachel Carter, Kate Sykes, and all of those who have been a part of this special writers community, you have inspired me and kept me pushing.

Thank you to my friends at Vermont Studio Center, the Lost River Writers Retreat, and all those who have given me a space to write. Thank you to the librarians and independent booksellers who make our communities richer. Thank you to all of the teachers and professors who encouraged me over the years, especially to Mary Morris for her guidance, as well as the other faculty and students at Sarah Lawrence College.

Thank you to all the editors who have given my work a home, including many of the stories herein.

Thank you to all of my friends and family for supporting me, notably Kelsey Goodson Dunn for keeping me laughing all these years, Ali Vigneau Ewald for your constant support, and Chelsea Mandigo for your lifelong friendship; Brian Sheffer for always checking in and celebrating my successes (with book mail!); and Jess Mizzi for all the love. Thank you to my beloved aunts, Lori Kilburn and Diane McAllister, for so much, including your constant support, and to all the Kilburns, Nichols's, and Frazers for your love. To my parents, for giving me every opportunity, encouraging my passion for reading and writing, and putting books in my hands. To my brother Mac for being such a valuable part of my support system. And most especially, thank you to Dylan, my loving husband, without whom nothing I do would be possible. I like you and I love you.

Finally, to Arden; you have my whole heart.

Thank you to the editors who selected the following stories for publication, some in earlier versions:

"Ember," *Lunate*, 2019. Nominated for a Pushcart Prize.

"Chopped," *Idle Ink*, 2022.

"Family Secret" ("Family Portrait), *Lunate*, 2020.

"Hands," *Burningword Literary Journal*, 2020.

"Love Lines," *Emerge Literary Journal*, 2022.

"No One Will Ever Hear You," *Noir Nation*, 2020. Winner of Golden Fedora Fiction Prize.

"The Bra Tree," *Bright Flash Literary Review*, 2021.

"THIS IS NOT A DRILL," *Literary Orphans,* 2019.

"When You Are Not Home" and "How We Feed Ourselves," *Runaway Parade*, 2014.

"Yes, but." *Bloodroot Literary Magazine*, 2021.

Author Bio

Erika Nichols-Frazer is the author of the memoir *Feed Me: A Story of Food, Love and Mental Illness* and the poetry collections *Staring Too Closely* and *Can you see her, the moon?* She has been editor of several anthologies, including the mental health recovery anthology, *A Tether to This World.* She has published more than thirty short stories, essays, and poems in literary journals such as *River Teeth's Beautiful Things, Gone Lawn, Emerge Literary Journal, Burningword Literary Journal, Lunate, HuffPost,* and others. She has an MFA from the Bennington Writing Seminars and a BA from Sarah Lawrence College.

Nichols-Frazer is a former journalist and freelance writer; dozens of her articles have appeared in publications across Vermont, New England, and the US. Nichols-Frazer also owns Good Wolf Literary Services and previously worked as a developmental editor for New Degree Press.

She has spoken publicly about writing and mental health and taught writing in a variety of settings. She works at Vermont State University and lives in Central Vermont with her family and various animals. Visit her website www.nicholsfrazer.com.

www.ingramcontent.com/pod-product-compliance
Lightning Source LLC
Chambersburg PA
CBHW032305250826
50436CB00030B/266
9781578692309